A MAN OF MYSTERY

Eleanor was a bit surprised at the luxury of Griff's carriage and matched grays, the soft fur robes lined with cashmere. He was not only well dressed but his equipage spoke of an old and honored family with considerable resources. Before, he had been plain Mr. Preston, though she had known his father was an earl, of course. Why had he never come back to renew his suit? Weeks later she heard he had gone off to the Peninsula. Her dreams about him for the past six years might have created a person rather unlike what he actually was.

It seemed to her that Griff was very good at this Society business. For a man who had once claimed to be such an outsider, so disgusted with the nonsensical pretensions and arrogances of the *ton,* he bore the trappings well. Either he had changed in his outlook or he was an accomplished charlatan. Neither role seemed possible for the man she loved, a man who now seemed only a figment of her imagination. . . .

MISS MILFORD'S MISTAKE

Victoria Hinshaw

ZEBRA BOOKS
Kensington Publishing Corp.
http://www.kensingtonbooks.com

ZEBRA BOOKS are published by

Kensington Publishing Corp.
850 Third Avenue
New York, NY 10022

First Printing: November 2003
10 9 8 7 6 5 4 3 2 1

Printed in the United States of America

To the memory of Edward Barnard Metcalf
(1783-1850),
Royal Draughtsman and Surveyor,
my great-great-great-grandfather,
and to all his descendants in Britain,
North America, and Australia

One

Miss Eleanor Milford stopped briefly before the mirror in the kitchen hallway to repin her chestnut curls. She could hear the bustle of the maid setting out the teapot and muttering ominously from the vicinity of the stove. The dowager duchess, Eleanor's grandmother, was in the drawing room, the first time in years that her grace had come here to the modest home of her second son in Branden-under-Wrotham.

There wasn't time for Eleanor to change into something more becoming than the sprigged muslin she wore to teach the village girls in the remodeled shed out back. Giving her hair one last futile pat, she straightened her shoulders and stood tall. Whatever the dowager had on her mind, it was probably not her granddaughter's clothing. Eleanor prayed her grandmother had not come to express her wrath at learning of the existence of the school, for her students had truly grown to be the most important matter in Eleanor's life.

When Eleanor entered the drawing room, the dowager seemed to be appraising the quality of the draperies with less than approval, a look of distaste on her wrinkled countenance.

"Good afternoon, Grandmother." Eleanor closed

the door behind her and met the dowager's gaze head on.

Her grandmother peered down her long nose, looking Eleanor up and down as though she were assessing the worth of a new lapdog. "Come over here and sit down, young lady. You look disgraceful, Eleanor. Like a dairymaid or a laundress."

Eleanor followed the instructions, stifling a grin at the error of her previous expectation. Grandmother never missed a blemish in anything she encountered. At least the furniture had a fresh coat of polish and the lamp chimneys were sparkling.

The dowager, wearing a sober black gown in the fashion of the last century, waved a hand at her long-suffering companion. "Wait for me outside, Mason. Tell John to walk the horses."

When Mason was gone, the dowager pursed her lips and frowned as she raised her quizzing glass for a better view. "Now that I see what a lamentable hoyden you have become, I wonder if you will do."

"I was about to say what an unusual pleasure it is for me to welcome you." Eleanor put on her sweetest smile.

"Fustian! Do not try to humor me." With a shrug, the dowager released the eyeglass. "There is no one else to accomplish this stratagem, so you will have to rise to the occasion."

"The occasion?"

"Priscilla's presentation. You will accompany her and that peagoose Violet to London next week. Later, I shall come myself for the Queen's Drawing Room and the ball, but I expect you to oversee all the preparations and take her to the proper gatherings."

"Grandmother, I cannot possibly leave Father alone."

"Nonsense! I will not be defied, Eleanor. Priscilla is spoiled and headstrong. Violet makes no pretense of control, and she will no doubt take to her bed with a megrim most days. What Lawrence was thinking of when he married that empty-headed ninny I have never perceived. She is quite insufficient as the Duchess of Branden. But that is neither here nor there. Priscilla is the youngest of my grandchildren, and she must have a suitable Season."

Lawrence, the seventh Duke of Branden and Eleanor's uncle, had married the fragile Violet only a few years ago. Secretly, Eleanor agreed with her grandmother's assessment. The new duchess, younger than her oldest stepchild by several years, had neither the disposition nor the accomplishments to fulfill her obligations, and her beauty had already given way to plump indolence.

"But certainly one of my aunts could help. Or Priscilla's sister, Prudence."

"Prudence is increasing again. As for my daughters, I assume they have responsibilities elsewhere. You are at hand, and I see no reason why you should oppose the task. After all, you have not been in London for several years. You should welcome the occasion to renew your acquaintances."

Eleanor had no desire ever again to visit Town, but that was not the most compelling reason to resist her grandmother. The only way Uncle Lawrence had allowed her to start the school was to keep the dowager from knowing about it. She didn't believe in education for females. Amalia, Dowager Duchess of Branden, could hardly read or

write herself. Mason handled her extensive correspondence. Eleanor had never seen the dowager
with a book in hand nor heard her comment on
anything other than the fashion plates in the ladies'
magazines.

"I shall take this up with Father at dinner."

The dowager vigorously shook her head, dis-
lodging a hairpin from her elaborate coiffure. She
jabbed it back in place at once. "Where is he? Out
wandering in the shrubbery, I suppose."

"I do not know . . ."

Molly entered with a tray bearing the best china
cups. "Yer papa is in the library, Miss."

"Fetch him, Eleanor, while I see what I can do
with this tea."

As she rose, Eleanor felt her shoulders slump.
Her father would never defy his mother, no matter
what inconvenience she caused. She hoped to convince him later to let her stay in Hertfordshire, but
faced with the dowager's domineering presence, he
would not hesitate to accommodate her wishes.

Eleanor peeked into the library and motioned to
her father. "Grandmother wishes to speak to you."

He put down his quill, looked up from his man-
uscript, and grimaced. "I hoped she would think I
was out."

"Molly gave you away. But if you sneak out
through the terrace, I may truthfully say you have
gone."

"What does she want?" He moved quickly to the
side door.

"Something to do with Violet and Priscilla."

"What the deuce! They are entirely Lawrence's
concern. I need none of that."

"Then hurry." Eleanor watched him disappear outside.

She took her time returning to the drawing room.

Griffith Preston, Baron Bromley, rolled up his meticulously drawn map and stared over the valley of Ribblesdale. His carriage was waiting, but he wanted to engrave this lovely view upon his memory before he finished his last job as a Royal Draughtsman and Surveyor. The sky shaded from deep azure to a silvery blue at the horizon. The meandering river wound its careless way through golden fields and past clumps of trees so dark they were nearly black. From now on, the existence he had known for six years would be only a memory.

He did not relish his future as the heir to his family's estates and dwindling fortune. That the eventual responsibilities of an earl of the realm had meant little to his late brother only emphasized the irony of fate. Griff had gone off to war and survived; James waged battle only upon the gaming tables of London or in meaningless curricle races, one of which had cost him his life. James's death had driven their father ever deeper into dementia. His mother had a new fixation—making sure he, Griff, found a wife to fill his nursery, and soon!

Griff knew he should be grateful he was able to complete the government contracts in Yorkshire before going back to his childhood home in Sussex to take over the estates. In fact, he would rather make maps, as he had in the Peninsula and in Belgium with Wellington's army.

Since the end of the war, he had learned to

appreciate the subtleties of Britain's landscape, re-fining the maps drawn decades ago. He had the skill, the accuracy, and the temperament to make every detail perfect. Living in tents or in village inns with a few associates suited him well.

Now that life was over. He would have to content himself with making maps of his new irrigation ditches and paddock fences. Or whatever his new duties would bring.

Then there was the matter of finding a suitable wife. He had no hope of finding love. He had once tried, and the resulting regret at losing her still haunted his memories. No, love was not to be an in-gredient of the match. In fact, his mother would most likely choose the young lady who would even-tually succeed her as Countess of Edenhurst. She would concentrate on the most important qualities of a potential bride, rather than allow Griff's ten-dency to compare every female he met with the chestnut-haired, blue-eyed beauty to whom he had lost his heart. And for whom he still yearned.

He stared over the peaceful valley and squared his shoulders. The road before him was clear, and he pledged himself to accept all the responsibilities of his new life. *I may be a fish out of water to begin with, but I shall learn to run the estate as well as I have mapped this terrain.*

Eleanor paced the small classroom, now empty of children, while her fellow teacher, Jane Wil-son, daughter of the vicar, watched with eyes full of concern.

"Jane, I am beside myself with irritation. Grandmother has ordered me to London for the Season to supervise Priscilla's come-out."

"The Prima?" Jane used the title they had secretly concocted to describe Eleanor's missish young cousin. "I wondered what the dowager duchess was up to."

"It is beyond anything. I am so distracted I feel like I should run away—escape and never return."

"What is wrong with the Prima's stepmama? Should she not be the one to see to her step-daughter's come-out?"

Eleanor stopped and fumbled with her hair ribbon. "Violet is a widgeon or, to my thinking, simply too slothful to concern herself with another person's needs for more than a moment."

"If the dowager has decided, I suppose there is no recourse. Unless your father can convince . . ."

She resumed her steps. "Oh, Jane, Papa will not express a word of dissent. Nothing trumps the dowager's whims."

"Norrie!" Jane's horrified tone belied her wide smile.

"Oh, you know what I mean. She says Priscilla is spoiled, but no one compares to the way Grand-mother imposes herself on others. I have not consented yet, and I will do my best to resist."

"But you should be happy to return to London for a visit. There must be many changes since you were last there."

"Perhaps enough to interest me for a week or two, but for a stay of several months? In a way, I can hardly blame Violet for falling into a decline at the thought of Town."

"You might run into some of your old suitors."

At last Eleanor drooped into a chair. "Pray that I do not. Nothing would be more distasteful, unless they are married with a passel of children underfoot. The very last thing I need in my life is a man who would question my desire to teach our girls and boys."

Jane had a dreamy look in her eyes. "Not even if you saw that one fellow you rather favored, Norrie?"

Eleanor feigned nonchalance. "If he was not lost in a battle somewhere, he has probably gone to India or the colonies."

"Following the suggestion of your mother, as I recall."

"That was a half dozen years ago. I have not thought of him for ages." Only every time the familiar fragrance of lavender mixed with roses, or when she looked at the faded flowers she had pressed in her diary. Then the face of Griffith Preston made her heart race and her eyes begin to water. These were troubling reactions, and Eleanor did her best to suppress them.

"You might meet someone new."

"Jane, I would be only a chaperon for the Prima. I would be busy trying to keep her from disgracing the family. Anyway, today's men are seeking chits just out of the schoolroom. Many are the fellows who think they can mold a wife to their wishes before she is flawed by gaining interests of her own. From my observations, this is a fallacious assumption. But be assured no one would bother with someone of my age. At twenty-five, I have been on the shelf for ages."

"You are foolish to think you will not attract any admirers, Norrie."

"La, Jane, you have no notion how feeble are my charms."

"If I were you, I should welcome an escape from my ordinary life."

Eleanor suddenly recognized the undercurrent in the conversation. "Why did I not think of it before? If I have to go, you can come for a visit. The dowager duchess and the duke will be in London for Priscilla's presentation to the Queen and for her ball. Then they would leave me to chaperon her other merriments while the vanishing Violet attends to her precious nerves. You could keep me company for a while. We might see all the sights of London, and perhaps between the two of us, we could keep the Prima from betraying her true nature as a self-centered twit, thus destroying any hope of a suitable match."

Jane's face lit up. "Do you mean I could stay at Branden House?"

"Of course you could. There are at least a dozen bedchambers. You can accompany me to balls, dinners, musical afternoons, and . . ."

"But I could not attend any parties."

"Why not? You are delightfully accomplished. You might even play the harp for a gathering."

"Norrie, I would have nothing to wear. I should be confined to the house or I would embarrass you, not to mention Priscilla."

"We are about the same size. If I go up to town and order my own wardrobe, I could simply order a few things to compliment your dark hair and eyes. The Dowager says she will provide everything. She will broach no interference with dressing her granddaughters in the latest mode. No one would

blink if I ordered twelve dresses instead of six. In
fact, I could have twenty made, and there would be
no complaints. But I am not promising anything
yet. I must pay my usual obeisance at the dowager's
Thursday Afternoon. I shall mount a last stand."

Jane squeezed her hand. "I must not fib to you,
Norrie. I am just as selfish as the Prima. I hope your
battle will be lost."

Arriving at the Dower House precisely at four, the
appointed hour for her grandmother to receive her
daughters, granddaughters, and nieces, Eleanor
greeted seven of her relations with the expected
compliments to their ensembles, all of which exhibited homage to the coming spring. Indeed, the
drawing room resembled a flower garden of pastel
hues, as well as a dressmaker's catalogue of frills,
flounces, and fringes.

According to her usual practice, Eleanor's dress
could not have been remotely considered a com-
petitor in the Thursday rivalry for the highest
approbation of the gathering, though she had
taken considerable care to appear above reproach.
Her peach-colored silk did not rise to the latest in
design, but the matching ribbons woven through
her shiny chestnut hair managed to garner a word
of praise from Aunt Sophy.

The chattering stopped for a moment when
Priscilla and Violet hurried in, always the last ones
to arrive. Eleanor was not surprised to see her
cousin arrayed in a shell-pink confection with
enough trimmings to adorn three or four less over-
loaded and more tasteful garments. Violet looked

pale and clasped her reticule tightly to her bosom. No doubt the bag was full of headache powders, hartshorn, and several vinaigrettes to see her through the next half hour.

When the butler announced the dowager, all stood and curtsied in precisely the manner her grace preferred. Eleanor never failed to find amusement in the old-fashioned formality of the proceeding, repeated nearly every week of the year in the manner of a Royal Court, though everyone present was related by blood or marriage and lived within two miles of one another.

As always, the dowager spoke first. "Priscilla will make her formal entry into Society this year. Violet and Eleanor will spend the Season with her in London."

A chorus of "ahs" greeted her comment.

"I myself shall present her to the Queen. All of you will attend her ball at Branden House in April."

Eleanor felt a twinge in the pit of her stomach. Of course Grandmother thought she was going to London, as instructed. But did she have to tell everyone already? She let the conversation buzz about her, nodding here and there to the few comments sent in her direction.

All of them considered her peculiar to have shunned the *haut ton* for so many years. They no longer enquired about her aspirations, and she knew that behind her back they rolled their eyes and threw up their hands. None of them had the slightest sympathy with a woman who chose to remain unmarried. Not even cousin Olivia, who had mourned for five years after her betrothed died aboard one of the first ships sending troops to

Portugal, saw Eleanor's reluctance to wed as anything but demented. Olivia had finally settled for an older man and claimed delight in her four stepchildren and two infants of her own, as she rarely abstained from reminding Eleanor.

The dowager's traditional style of pouring the tea never failed to bring declarations of admiration from her fawning onlookers. Eleanor vacillated between annoyance and hilarity at the antics of the ladies, all vying for a higher place on the fabled list of legatees Grandmother did not mention directly but kept in play by frequent innuendoes sprinkled through her conversations. When Eleanor accepted her teacup, the dowager caught her eye. "Please remain when the others have left."

"Yes, Grandmother."

Even this insignificant exchange swiveled heads in Eleanor's direction for a moment.

Lady Prudence guided Eleanor to a settee where they sat side by side.

"I offer my felicitations, Cousin," Eleanor said.

Prudence heaved a great sigh. "I cannot say I am ecstatic at having another child so soon. But Perry has great hopes for a male this time, and so do I."

"Naturally." Eleanor thought Prudence quite fortunate to have three little girls who tended to resemble her instead of their rather frog-faced father.

"I am so happy you will be in London with Priscilla. Violet . . ." Prudence broke off to gaze upon her stepmother, who was patting her heart as she talked to Aunt Sophy. "Look at her, pretending to be at death's door. She is the saddest excuse for a proper wife I can imagine. Father must rue the day he ever laid eyes on her."

Eleanor took a small sip of the Bohea. "Perhaps, but I do admire his steadfastness. I have never heard him utter an unflattering word about her."

"He would not dare! Under that simpering exterior, she has a heart of stone and a Trojan's temper. Whatever you do in London, do not cross her."

"To be honest, I have not actually agreed to Grandmother's plans."

"You have a choice?"

Eleanor laughed wryly. "Probably not."

"I cannot imagine why you are not eager to go."

"I have my . . ." She stopped herself before she mentioned the school.

Prudence lifted her cup to her lips and sniffed. "Nasty stuff, this."

"I believe Grandmother is still brewing from the supply she received as a wedding gift sixty-some years ago."

"Eleanor, while you are keeping one eye on Priscilla, find yourself a husband. Just think, you might marry a man who lives in the Antipodes, and then you would be free of these wretched Thursdays."

"My dear Prudence, you may have a point there." Smiling, Eleanor took Prudence's cup and carried the two offending potions to a side table.

The room emptied within another quarter hour, and Eleanor prepared herself to argue with the dowager, never an activity to engender confidence in one's success.

When the footman had removed the tea tray, Eleanor sat in the chair next to her Grandmother and hoped her mood would not turn waspish.

The dowager rubbed her hands together as if

ridding herself of all traces of her relatives. "Mason has a list for you, Eleanor. There are matters you must attend to before you leave, with some to be accomplished within your first weeks in Town. I will send orders for the house to be opened before your arrival."

"Grandmother, I do not wish to leave Father alone, nor do I feel qualified to manage Priscilla's Season. I cannot . . ."

"Rubbish! Do not think I am unable to recall your Seasons. You were quite the Toast, is that not true?"

"But, I . . ."

"Do not interrupt. You comported yourself admirably, for the most part. You received several quite respectable offers, which you inexplicably rejected. If your mother had not been so foolish to catch a nasty chill and expire well before her time, she would have had you appropriately wed to someone fitting to your station. I daresay you would not have defied both of us for long."

Eleanor nodded, for the dowager spoke the truth. It was only after her mother died that Eleanor saw her future in a different light, not as the appendage of a husband, but as an independent woman.

"She should not have left you so generous a portion. Money belonging to a girl too young only spoils her and gives her nonsensical ideas unsuitable for a granddaughter of the Duke of Branden."

So the dowager blamed her mother for Eleanor's situation! "I will not have you speak ill of my mother and her intentions."

Surprisingly, the dowager seemed to soften her tone. "I want only what is best for all my granddaughters. I have lived a long time, Eleanor, and I have seen the generations come and go in several noble families. I am a better judge of what young women need, my dear, than you shall be for at least another three or four decades. But be that as it may, my primary concern is Priscilla. You may have the sense to make the best of your spinsterhood, but she would not. Nor is she capable of judging who is and who is not a proper match for herself."

In spite of her opposition to the dowager's plans, Eleanor had to agree Priscilla's future would be a problem. "I believe this, Grandmother: You are by far the best choice to superintend her entry into the marriage mart."

"I am not up to spending the entire Season in town. I am not a hypochondriac like Violet, but I am old and my joints are not what they were."

"But surely if you explained to Violet how Priscilla's success would enhance her own standing and please Uncle Lawrence . . ."

"Do not talk like a flibbertigibbet. You know very well that Violet lacks the capacity to see logic. Lawrence was a fool when he plucked her out of her first appearance at Almack's and carried her off in a trice. He did not wait long enough to see beyond those honey curls to her empty head. Of course, her mother had not an ounce of sense either, so I can only be gratified that Violet never spawned a child. I could not bear to see the Branden name attached to such an abomination."

"Grandmother!" Eleanor grabbed her handkerchief to smother her laughter.

"Well you may be amused. But now you understand the depths of my concern. Since Violet arrived, Priscilla has been without any direct guidance. She pays my advice no heed whatsoever, and I cringe to imagine how she would appear in the *ton* unless she has a level head beside her."

"But I am not that person."

"Look here, young lady. You will do as I say. I know what you and the vicar's daughter are up to."

"What?" Eleanor swallowed and drew a deep breath. This indeed was unexpected.

"You know that nothing occurs in this neighborhood without my knowledge. I do not approve of your whims, but I prefer not to interfere as long as it amuses you. However, if you defy my tactics for Priscilla's come-out, I shall see that no further school claptrap is ever heard again."

Eleanor bristled at the outright challenge. "I did not believe you would stoop to threats."

"My husband taught me a useful epigram that his own father acknowledged. 'The end must justify the means.' In this case, it applies quite appropriately."

Eleanor's heart pounded and she forced back a lump in her throat. "You would truly deny the children a chance to learn to read and write?"

"Unnecessary for most of them, who will merely take up ideas above their station. But I will not allow *you* to teach them unless you agree to my plans."

"That is cruel!"

The dowager made no answer. Her countenance was as composed and commanding as always. Eleanor struggled to remain calm while her mind spun with instant defiance. *This cannot be happening!*

Eleanor could not think of a single word to say. She stood and walked to the window, looking out over the peaceful park. The thought of losing her pitiful little efforts to help the children made her want to cry. But how could she give her Grandmother such satisfaction? The older girls had just sewn curtains for the rather crooked windows the boys cut in the old shed. She and Jane had sneaked off to the village to buy more slates and chalk. To think of losing all the smiles each morning . . .

She had been defeated by a master of the game indeed. But she still might salvage something.

She returned to her chair. "If I take on Priscilla's Season, will you provide us a decent place for the school?"

It was the dowager's turn to grimace. "Now you are trying to bargain with me?"

"Yes. The means to an end, I believe you said?"

The dowager gave a bark of laughter. "Eleanor, you show the mark of your grandfather!"

"Do you agree?"

"On one condition. I want Priscilla betrothed by June. To someone I would approve of. I'll have none of these dandies or fortune hunters. It will not be simple, Eleanor, but I believe you have just shown you have the perspicacity to succeed."

"So you will have your sojourn in London, Jane." Eleanor completed her account of the dowager's tête-à-tête as the two friends sat before the fire in the vicarage.

"Yes. And we will have a new school for the children."

"Sadly, that remains to be seen. First, I have to find some sapskull who is susceptible to Priscilla the Prima's questionable charms."

"She is pretty enough." Jane's statement was almost a question.

"Unless one admires sense. She has no accomplishments whatsoever. Foremost among her questionable attributes is a complete lack of self-discipline."

"Certainly she must play the pianoforte."

"Not a note. Perhaps I can find her a foreigner who knows no English."

"Norrie, would the dowager stand for that?"

"Probably not, unless he was particularly obsequious. And rich besides. He would have to have an impressive title and a distinguished heritage."

"Certainly not a Frenchman or a Russian. Perhaps a Swede or a Dane?"

"I can see it now. Count Viking von Stockholm, tall, handsome, and blond, whispering, 'My little *flicka*' in her delicate ear. She would probably slap him."

Jane giggled. "How about a dashing raven-haired Spaniard, sighing '*buena senorita*' or something like that?"

"Sounds promising. But what such a one would be doing at Almack's is the question."

"He might instruct young ladies in the art of playing the lute."

"You will not find me at any music master's. If I have to subject myself to preparing the Prima for a performance of some kind, I shall give up our school immediately and enter a nunnery in the highest reaches of the Alps."

"Don't forget the yodelers who inhabit that region, out calling for their goats."

Eleanor laughed, then adopted a pout. "Jane,

how dare you best me for the second time today? Have some regard for my wounds."

"I apologize. I had no idea you were so browbeaten."

"I shall try to look on the sunny side of the situation. What colors do you prefer for your new gowns? I heard someone chirping this afternoon about the latest hue. She called it 'aureolin,' and from the context I imagine it to be some shade of yellow."

"Which will make my complexion sickly green. But truly, Eleanor, I cannot allow you to buy me clothing."

"So call them a loan. At Branden House there will be maids who excel at altering dresses. In my first year in London, I had to have three gowns let out when I indulged in too many Viennese pastries for a few weeks. I even had to buy new slippers."

"There, think of that. My feet are much larger than yours." Jane held up her left leg. "As dainty as a plough-horse hoof."

"Never worry, dear Jane. When we embark upon this caper, we shall take all the time we need to find dancing slippers for you, no matter what the size."

"I shall begin working on Mama this very evening."

Eleanor's love for teaching had developed accidentally, entirely the result of circumstance. Mere weeks after she refused Griff's offer, her mother fell ill, and Eleanor returned home to Branden to nurse her. The dowager sent her cook, Mrs. Tibbits, to their house in Branden-under-Wrotham to help take care of her second son, his ill wife, and their daughter.

Over the months, as they often sat at the bedside of Fanny, Lady Harley, Mrs. Tibbits confided to

Eleanor her concern about her grandson Will. The boy, age twelve at the time, was particularly bright.

Jane Wilson, daughter of the vicar, tried to convince her father to include the boy in the group of lads he tutored in preparation for Eton, but Mr. Wilson believed Will's background was inappropriate for associating with the sons of the local gentry. Too smart for them, Jane had observed.

Before long, Eleanor and Jane themselves tutored the boy whose appreciation brought Eleanor strong satisfaction. Will's desire to learn about modern history, geography, and mathematics drove her to deepen her own knowledge.

The experience inspired Eleanor and Jane to invite other children of the estate workers and villagers to attend the classes they arranged, from learning their ABCs to *Lives of the Monarchs*. Jane held a newly minted certificate from a respected academy for young ladies. As Lady Harley continued to decline, slowly but steadily, teaching gave Eleanor's life some purpose, a reason to go on each day, and it enabled her to keep cheery as she tended to her mother and tried to boost the spirits of her father.

Eleanor had tried to keep knowledge of the school from the dowager, for she was known not to favor such exploits. But she was not really surprised that the old duchess knew everything. Many on the huge estate kept her informed, without question.

The more she taught, the more she wanted to teach, Eleanor found. The accomplishments of her students gave her immense pleasure. Opening young minds became her lifework, and she loved every minute of it. Only the possibility of the dowager or the duke ending the practice gave her worry.

If she succeeded with Priscilla, found her a match this year, Eleanor knew the dowager would honor her promise to back the school. The effort would take her away to London for months, but the reward was well worth her time and energy.

Two

Eleanor chose Tuesday's Belfour musicale for Lady Priscilla's first venture into London Society. Lady Belfour was famous for her musicales, always with the highest quality singers and artists, never overcrowded or uncomfortably overheated. The gathering would be small, a select audience of no more than fifty people, all innately respectable, all positively inclined to welcome the daughter of their dear friend, His Grace the Ninth Duke of Branden. Lady Belfour always provided estimable entertainment, allowing time for decorous conversation, followed by seating in the music room, a performance, then a light supper. They would be home well before midnight.

As Eleanor expected, Violet was far too fatigued to attend, needful of several days' lassitude to recover from her one shopping expedition. Her absence would make it easier to focus attention on Priscilla. Few of Violet's thoughts and certainly none of her utterances concerned anything but herself, making Eleanor more than content to leave the Duchess of Branden behind and deliver her excuses to Lady Belfour.

Before they left, Priscilla won Violet's approval for her ensemble.

Lying on her chaise in the sitting room, her vinaigrette at hand, Violet gave Priscilla an appraising look. "You look just right, my dear."

Eleanor agreed, secretly thinking her cousin looked sweeter and more demure than usual in her ivory gown trimmed in blond lace.

Violet heaved a great sigh. "I so wish I could accompany you, but I fear my spasms would . . ." She paused for dramatic effect. "I know Eleanor will introduce you to everyone."

As Violet weakly hugged Priscilla, Eleanor stole a look at herself in a large mirror. She had spent considerable time dressing, wishing to look mature enough to be a chaperon, yet disliking the thought of looking like a staid matron. In the end, she had chosen a gown of lime green trimmed in white silk roses. More white roses were anchored in her upswept hair. She would be on display too, for already she had heard rumors that a few old hens had speculated on her qualifications to direct her cousin's introduction to Society. Mrs. Chandler had whispered so when she called yesterday, ostensibly to meet Priscilla, more probably to pass along exactly that gossip.

The Branden town coach delivered them to the Belfour mansion. Eleanor shrugged off her concerns as they reached the door of the music room. The Prima dipped a very creditable curtsy to Lady Belfour, who greeted them both with delight.

"Lady Priscilla, my dear, we are so pleased to make your acquaintance, and honored to be among the first to have the pleasure of your company."

Priscilla looked rather surprised at the warmth of her reception. "The honor is mine, Lady Belfour."

Eleanor gave Lady Belfour a curtsy and a wide smile before her hostess drew her into an embrace.

"I am delighted to see you again, my dear."

"And I am pleased to be here."

Eleanor linked her arm through Priscilla's and drew her into the salon, away from the line of new arrivals coming up the stairs.

Side by side, they walked toward the other guests, many of whom turned to watch their approach. Eleanor hoped she would remember the names of those she had known in the past.

When Mrs. Shepperly waved to them, Eleanor gave Priscilla a little nudge in her direction. With pleasantries exchanged, compliments on all the ladies' apparel made, news of the health of the dowager duchess and other assorted acquaintances enumerated, Eleanor took her first look around the room. The decoration was a newer, brighter style than she recalled, with many more Gothic features.

She glanced back toward the door, where Lady Belfour welcomed more guests. The gentleman wearing buff pantaloons and a dark blue jacket who bowed over Lady Belfour's hand looked vaguely familiar. As he straightened up, Eleanor's breath froze.

Griffith Preston, the very last man she expected to see, stood across the room, as compelling in his appearance as she had ever seen him.

The years fell away as she stared at him, unable to take her eyes from his face. He smiled and spoke to Lady Belfour, but none of his words carried across the room to where she stood. His face was sun-touched, his hair as unruly as it had always been, refusing to submit to the brush or comb. His broad shoulders set him apart from most men.

He clasped his hands behind his back, a familiar habit that gave Eleanor's heart a jolt. Griff had stood exactly thus when he asked for her hand on May 14, almost six years ago. That was the moment Eleanor would never forget, the moment she had made the mistake of a lifetime.

She had gazed into his earnest gray eyes and then away for a moment before she voiced her words of refusal, carelessly uttered them, without consideration for the seriousness of the occasion. There in one instant she threw away the chance for love with a man she cared for. She had been a foolish flibbertigibbet. She simply disregarded the potential implications of her action, thus squelching the chance for the love of which most girls dreamed.

And why? Because she had been brainless and infantile, yet arrogant enough to assume he would ask again, probably several more times before she would accept. But he had not asked again. In fact, he had disappeared from London, and rumors said he had gone off to Portugal to join the British forces there.

Now, six years later, he stood across the room, as familiar as the face in her dreams, as welcome as a hornet in her boudoir. He was probably the sire of a growing brood, accompanied by a wife, though she saw no lady beside him, no companion of any kind.

Her heart pounded in her ears, drowning out the conversation nearby. Eleanor felt as though she were in a trance, a stupor of sorts. With great effort, she tried to regain control of her disorderly thoughts.

She pressed her cold hands together to still their shaking and hoped they would warm one another. Her skin was chilled, her pulse throbbing so hard she wondered that its rapidity did not warm her face and throat. She hoped all color had not drained from her face.

With great effort, she closed her eyes for an instant. Think of anything else, she chided herself. Ten minutes into their first social engagement of the Season and already she was shirking her duty.

Eleanor looked at Priscilla, who was entirely unfazed by Eleanor's momentary alarm, unaware the world had abruptly paused in its rotation. Forcing some measure of composure, Eleanor made herself attend to Mrs. Shepperly, who was nodding in Griff's direction.

"His elder brother died just over a year ago. He became Lord Bromley, heir to the Earl of Edenhurst. He has just arrived in town."

Eleanor almost gasped in astonishment. Griff was now a baron, his father's successor? This was completely unexpected, and if she remembered his thoughts accurately, a position he must detest. A chill ran up Eleanor's spine, and her throat tightened so she feared she could not speak. What would she do when they came face to face, as was bound to happen in a few moments? Surely he would recognize her. How should she greet him?

Only to Jane had she confided her regrets about her mistake. No one else, least of all the Prima, knew of her feelings about Griffith Preston. She had never told anyone they were even acquainted.

Much less that he had once kissed her.

Or that she dreamed of those kisses for six years.

Abruptly she felt a stiffening of her backbone. If she had her way, no one would ever know! She had long ago chosen her life without a man, other than in her fantasies. She intended to keep it that way.

Mrs. Shepperly went on. "He is eminently eligible, you know, Lady Priscilla. In fact, it is said he is seeking a wife."

When he approached, Eleanor could not keep her eyes from his face. In spite of her resolve, her heart fluttered dangerously, and she held herself rigid to prevent her anxiety from showing. The space he crossed took only a few of his long strides, though each one seemed to last forever. Her jaw muscles ached from the strain of holding her face expressionless.

Once he reached the three of them, the conversation passed quickly, sounding as if it came from afar in some foreign language. He made no special bow to her, only acknowledged their previous acquaintance with a solemn nod. She hardly heard the words they spoke, certain she mouthed the right phrases, yet none of them registered in her head.

She looked at him more closely, trusted herself to let her eyes feast on his face. He looked older, with a bit of crinkle around his eyes, yet it was most becoming. His eyes twinkled at Priscilla. With a stab of envy, Eleanor altered her gaze to take in her cousin's wide grin and fluttering eyelashes. How could he find it anything but childishly flirtatious, repulsively fawning? She clamped her teeth together and forced her lips to curve a little in some semblance of a smile.

Mrs. Shepperly carried on most of the conversation, relating the story of some exploit of her

daughter's. Time dragged on as Priscilla coyly simpered and Mrs. Shepperly chattered. Griff—Lord
Bromley, she would have to call him now—looked
back and forth between Priscilla and Mrs. Shepperly, seemingly enthralled with the girl, forbearing
of the older woman. Eleanor felt her chilly feet
were frozen to the floor.

"And so I told her I wished she would never do it
again. Of course she immediately tried it all over."

By the tone of her voice, Eleanor knew Mrs. Shepperly expected them to laugh, but the only sound
she could voice was a tiny chuckle, which sounded
tinny and false to her own ears. Lord Bromley had
the same deep rumbly laugh Eleanor had never forgotten. Hearing it again made her throat close up
and tears threaten. The Prima's giggle was drowned
out by Mrs. Shepperly's loud bray.

Eleanor felt as though she had been standing in
one place forever when the last of the guests filed
into the music room and two bewigged footmen directed them into chairs. Griff had moved toward the
rear of the room, out of sight. At last Eleanor could
relax her rigid spine and sink onto the gilt chair.

Priscilla grabbed her hand and whispered. "Did
you find Lord Bromley handsome, Norrie? I think
he is very good looking. Was I not all that was proper
to him?"

Eleanor blanched. "He is a fine gentleman,
Priscilla, and you were perfectly mannered."

Before she could say more, Lady Belfour came to
the front of the room to introduce the music.

Eleanor barely noticed her announcement, nor
did the notes that filled the air penetrate her consciousness. She felt anguish so deep she wished

only to sit in silence and filter out every sound, including the echoes of the bygone times filling her brain. Griff was a part of her past she never thought could recur. She needed time to gather her thoughts and recapture her tranquility. No one must ever know her feelings, for now she felt entirely foolish. The melodramatic fantasies that occupied too much of her imagination had been ridiculously mistaken.

She had not discovered she truly loved him until afterward, until she drove him away by refusing him, an act of rudeness she would regret forever.

Gradually her tension eased and her icy fingers warmed. Her thoughts unscrambled slowly and began to re-form into sensible truths. Griffith Preston was now Lord Bromley. She owed him her sympathy for his brother's death, a tragic loss for the family. Of all the men she had known, Griff was the most likely to loathe his new station, to detest being thrust into the status of heir to his father's earldom. Now he bore the entire burden of his family's future, something he had long ago told her he would hate. His cherished independence would be gone, replaced by the duties of managing the family estates and moving in circles of governmental responsibility.

When she had known him nearly six years ago, Griff never would have attended a *ton* party such as Lady Belfour's musicale. He would have laughed to think of himself perched on a little spindly chair surrounded by the stiffest doyennes in Mayfair and listening to violinists dressed in the powdered wigs and satin coats of the eighteenth century.

Part of her remained here in the music room.

Part of her tried to be far away, aloof from the proceedings. For two more quartets, she tamped down the ache in her heart, knowing that gradually she would have to build a barrier, a wall to keep her feelings secret.

She stared at the lovely ceiling, decorated with large medallions painted by Angelika Kaufmann. Nymphs and cupids and mythological lovers. Dare she think of spending time with him again? Could she rekindle his interest?

Griff took a seat in the last row. Why had he been so unprepared? He should have anticipated he might see Eleanor Milford in London, married or not. Perhaps he had been too comfortable with his belief that the woman he fell in love with six years ago was forever beyond his reach, mothering a family, as unattainable to him as if she lived on the moon.

He trusted his amazement had not been evident when he noticed Eleanor just a foot away, looking as luminously lovely as always. She might have been as stunned as he was, but when they exchanged a few words, she had been cool and collected.

He had feared meeting her eyes. He watched her only out of the corner of his eye, focusing his gaze beyond her shoulder or above her head.

Years ago, he had fallen completely and unexpectedly in love with Eleanor. The attention of his family had always been on his brother, the heir to the earldom, and his marriage prospects. James had delighted in spoiling all the potential plans of the mamas and their dear daughters who aspired to the role of countess. For Griff, it was a matter of an occasional dance with an occasional girl, often the ones James dangled, then dropped. No one—not his family, not the matchmaking mamas, not the title-seeking girls—cared what he, Griff, did. Perhaps this very lack of attention had made him even more vulnerable.

Thus it came as a surprise when he first met Eleanor and found her so agreeable. For several weeks, they encountered one another more and more frequently, until it became clear that their meetings were no accident. She was bright and clever, interested in everything from her father's collection of fossils to the King's collection of paintings, from new trees and flowers brought to England from faraway lands to the myths of ancient cultures. He thought she was fond of him beyond any other.

Eleanor had seemed different a few moments ago, her face lovely but lacking animation, like an etching in granite. She had never married. All those nights in Spain when he had tortured himself with thoughts of her in another's arms, none of that had happened. He could have spared himself eons of despondency.

What had she been doing for six years? Had someone broken her heart? Or had her brittle look come from within? What joys and disappointments had shaped her stony countenance?

Why had she declined his request to speak to her father? If he had not fled immediately, he might have found out. But what difference would knowing make now, except to assuage his curiosity?

Until he knew the answer, he could not throw off his feelings of betrayal. Back then he had no money, no future. Had she thought him, a mere second son, beneath her consideration? Now that he was his father's heir and would someday be the Earl of Edenhurst, she might have a different view.

When the applause after the final crescendo and closing chords signaled the end of the concert, Eleanor felt sure she could keep her dignity for the rest of the evening. She stood with Priscilla and moved toward the supper room, stopping to introduce her cousin to the Sandersons and their daughter Charlotte, with whom Priscilla might find some common interests.

Mrs. Sanderson declared her elation at the music, citing passage after passage that had inspired her rapture. Eleanor nodded her agreement. As she suspected, Priscilla and Miss Sanderson whispered together, ostensibly on their way to becoming fast friends. Eleanor took a step backward and looked to her left, trying to be as composed as any lady could be who wished to remain inconspicuous.

The garrulous tones of Jasper Hartselle's voice almost startled her. "My darling Cousin Eleanor. I am thrilled to have you back in Town! And dearest Cousin Priscilla! I am entirely at your service." He bowed low to them.

Hartselle, as he was known to the *ton*, was a distant cousin and, at the moment, a welcome distraction for Eleanor.

She dipped a curtsy. "Cousin Hartselle, I am pleased to see you here. I trust you are in good health?"

"My dear Eleanor, if I were to catalogue all my

complaints, we would have to stay the night, putting Lady Belfour to considerable trouble. I shall not regale you but say I endeavor to rise above my afflictions almost every day."

Eleanor responded with the laughter he expected. He might be the dandiest fribble in London, but he rarely failed to amuse her. Today he wore a yellow striped waistcoat and waved a lacy handkerchief as he spoke. His cheeks were rouged, his hair intricately curled and pomaded. His tail-coat of a shade of green much brighter than most gentlemen wore was decorated with brass buttons large enough to serve as platters. Hartselle truly cherished his position as best-dressed among his circle.

"Is the darling dowager duchess here? I have not seen her for at least three years."

Eleanor shook her head. "Not at the moment. She will arrive in a few weeks for Priscilla's presentation and for her ball. Only Priscilla and the duchess, her stepmama, and I are at Branden House."

"Ah, dearest Violet. She is suffering the megrims today?"

"As she does on most occasions, I fear."

Hartselle placed his hand on his heart. "As one who shares the liabilities of a delicate constitution, I know precisely how she feels."

Priscilla grasped Hartselle's hand to bring him into her conversation with Miss Sanderson.

Eleanor stepped back away from the group, eager for a moment's respite. She almost bumped into Griff and turned quickly.

He made a shallow bow. "Miss Milford, your servant."

She returned his courtesies. "Lord Bromley, it has been many years since we met."

"Years in which there have been many changes in our lives, Miss Milford. As you know, James was unexpectedly taken from us."

She nodded.

He continued. "A tragedy for my parents. A matter of great change for me, not much of it welcome, I fear.

"How is your mother after her appalling loss?"

"She arrived in Town today. She needs a bit of diversion after her mourning. Father is slipping ever more into vagueness. He still tries to keep the reins of the estates in hand, but he has no appetite for life."

"How very sad for him."

"Indeed it is. I must ask of your parents, Miss Milford. Are they well?"

"I lost my mother almost five years ago. Father is much the same, however, no more worldly than he ever was. I believe he is living the life you once expected, as the brother who does not need to look after the tenants or fulfill duties to the nation. He is content with his geographical interests, his collection of fossils, and his hens."

He nodded, giving her a solemn half smile. "I am sorry to hear about your mother."

"Thank you, Lord Bromley."

"I may never get used to that. Sounds like people are speaking to James."

"Yes." Eleanor had never felt more uncomfortable, giving and accepting sympathy in such a stilted manner.

"I quite expected you to be married with several children by now."

"I have several dozen children, to be honest." She noted his shocked look, a look that quickly changed to a grin.

"I know there is more to this story than you have told me."

"A friend and I have started a school for the tenants' children. I love teaching them."

"I am not surprised, Miss Milford. You have a talent for assisting others."

"I do?" Eleanor was surprised at his remark. "I should have thought you would consider me a complete ninnyhammer after the way I treated . . . I mean after the way I . . ." She let her voice fade away.

"I assure you, Miss Milford, I am none the worse for your treatment of me. I believe sincerely that young men ought to have several instances of disappointment before they reach real wisdom. It is excellent preparation for life's constraints."

Eleanor did not know what to say or what to think of his response. Did he mean he was glad she rejected him? Perhaps he considered his escape to be good fortune.

Before she had to reply, they were joined by Sir Gavin Gawthorpe, Hartselle, and Priscilla, and she found herself commenting on a performance she had barely heard.

Only when Priscilla asked where his family came from did a sudden stab of pain rouse Eleanor from her daze.

"My family comes from Edenhurst, a small place in Sussex."

The name of the place Eleanor had thought about so often she felt she had been there, wondering if he was there or far away, in England or abroad, even if he was alive or dead.

While the conversation flowed around her, Eleanor watched Griff out of the corner of her eye. She wished she knew what to think of his remark.

Eventually the circulation of the guests separated Griff from their group and brought back Mrs. Shepperly into a lively comparison of the first and third musical performances.

As Eleanor and Priscilla prepared to take their leave of Lady Belfour, Mrs. Shepperly leaned close and whispered, "It is said Bromley is looking for a wife. I think he might be a perfect match for you, Lady Priscilla."

Eleanor blanched. A match for the Prima? The words reverberated in her head. For Priscilla.

Eleanor tried to speak but her mouth felt dry. No words came out.

Priscilla cocked her head to one side and raised her eyebrows. "He is certainly very attractive."

Mrs. Shepperly prattled on. "I believe he is twenty-eight. The perfect age for you, Lady Priscilla."

Eleanor clenched her jaw and willed herself to silence. Griff and Priscilla? Impossible! A catastrophe!

Three

Griff slumped into a chair in his rooms and stared blindly at the carpet, angry at himself, at Eleanor, at fate. His feelings for her, so long suppressed and utterly unbearable, made him livid with rage. He had left all pretense of polite manners on the pavement in front of Lady Belfour's door. His solitary walk home had been punctuated by a muttered string of army curses he thought he had left behind on the battlefield.

He was not going to wallow in heated self-pity. He stood and shrugged out of his jacket, stripped off his cravat, rolled up his sleeves, and took out his sketchbook. He flipped the pages until he came to the plan for draining the farthest corner of Bromley Manor's western field. The neat precision of the lines he had drawn usually brought him comfort and solace in his low moments.

But staring at them now, he only saw Eleanor's smile and remembered his remark to her, intimating he had not suffered from her rejection. What a lie! But if he had his way, she would never know how much her refusal had hurt him, how on long nights under the starry skies of Portugal he had yearned for her and refused to give in to his repeated desire to cry out in pain.

He told himself he was too strong a man to fall to pieces over a lost romance. Many men of no more than half his inner strength had survived multiple loves and losses, if even a fraction of their stories were to be believed.

The only time he had ever shared his disappointment was when he and Bobby Bates were wounded in a skirmish in Spain, well ahead of their troops as they tried to map the terrain for forthcoming battles. Griff remembered every moment, every ache, every word.

When the enemy withdrew, they lay for hours in the silent darkness before he and Bobby began to whisper.

"How badly are you hurt, Bobby?" Griff had spoken softly, praying none of the enemy was left within earshot.

"Not bad. I am bloody but not injured much more than a flesh wound, I figure. You?"

"Just about the same. My hand might be broken from my fall, and there is a chunk missing from my thigh."

Bobby moaned a bit as he shifted position. "I expect they will come back in the morning and finish us off."

"No doubt."

"Do you think we could drag ourselves into a better spot, a safer place?"

Griff gave a sarcastic chuckle. "Which direction would that be? I cannot see anything, nor do I know what direction we should move if we get our bearings. Our troops were to the west, but if the French overran them, who knows where they went? All I know is that I am damned cold lying here."

"As cold as a woman who won't surrender a kiss."

Griff snorted and gave a half laugh. "I assume you speak from experience, my friend."

"And from the tone of your laugh I assume you, too, have known the chill of an indifferent female."

"To tell the truth, I have been unlucky in love."

"With your looks and family, Griff? Unlucky? I doubt you have tried very hard."

"Perhaps not. And you, Bobby?"

"I have equivocated every time I found someone I favored. Not a way to endear oneself to a woman. Have you ever been in love?"

It might have been the cold, the pain, or the prospect of the French troops returning to kill them that loosened Griff's tongue. He confessed to Bobby all his love for Eleanor and how she had fobbed him off when he asked her if he could speak to her father.

Bobby reciprocated with several tales of young ladies he had once courted but had never decided upon finally. "That feeling of wanting to spend forty or fifty years with one woman never caught my fancy."

"I was prepared to spend an eternity with Miss Milford, but she obviously did not share my view."

And so they had spent the cold and wretched night. As dawn slowly slid over their resting place, the troops that appeared were part of their own familiar British regiments. Neither Griff nor Bobby had serious wounds; neither spent much time in surgeons' tents. Neither again mentioned their intimate conversation, Griff being thoroughly embarrassed about his admission of lost love.

Griff stared again at the simple map before him.

He ought to grab his horse and ride straight back to Bromley this very minute. What the devil? He was not cut out for musicales or courting young ladies. Let his mother pick some girl and bring her to him.

"Blast and damn!" He almost cried out the words. That busybody Shepperly woman would have sent a note to her dear friend Lady Edenhurst the minute she arrived home from the musicale. Mother would know all about Lady Priscilla, the daughter of a duke. Mother knew nothing of his old feelings for Eleanor, and certainly she knew nothing of his contradictory feelings now.

Griff wished for the thousandth time he was in the muddy fields lugging a hundred pounds of surveying instruments instead of adorning the stone pavements of St. James's Street carrying only a pair of tan driving gloves and a foppish walking stick. He felt like a fool, masquerading as a man of fashion, entirely out of his element.

It was a devilish truth that Eleanor still appealed to him. He had been broadsided by her calm beauty and icy poise a few hours ago. Yet he had almost insulted her, had he not? His hurt and confusion had spilled over in an unsavory remark he should have repressed. Even after six years, the sting of her rejection and the lack of explanation were alive and well in his heart

For the last few years he was a man on the road, always traveling, moving from one place to another and liking the life. But that was behind him now. A wife would be part of the new Griffith. If his mother's choice was Lady Priscilla Branden, why not accede to her wishes? Eleanor had looked so untouched that he doubted his old feelings had disturbed a hair on her head. *Whoops, my man, getting tetchy again.*

He closed his sketchbook. Griff knew the coming day would test his mettle indeed. Might as well have been back in the mountains of Spain.

Fitful dreams spoiled Eleanor's sleep, and she performed her morning ablutions inattentively. Only when she was alone in her bedchamber after breaking her fast did she allow her thoughts to go back to the significance of Griff's remarks as she brushed her hair. Clearly Griff had given her a set-down, though one she admittedly deserved. Perhaps she should write him a note, try to explain.

With a tap at the door, Priscilla came in. "Eleanor, may I ask you a question? Do you think grandmother would approve of Lord Bromley?"

Eleanor swallowed hard and forced a smile onto her face. "He will be an earl. His status is certainly acceptable. Did Grandmother say she expects you to marry a duke, my dear?"

"No. Charlotte told me there are no dukes looking for wives, not a single one."

"Did she also say there were no first sons of dukes in the marriage mart?" Eleanor prayed there were several whom Priscilla could pursue.

"Her mother says not a single heir apparent. Perhaps two or three who are grandsons."

"Sufficient for your purposes, are they not? You come from an excellent background, so you may aspire high."

"I thought Lord Bromley quite attractive. Do you think he is too old for me?"

"Certainly not." Eleanor almost snapped the words and she forced her voice to a quieter tone. "You do not want to marry a man who is immature, Priscilla."

"Do you know how old Bromley is?"

Eleanor knew precisely how old Griff was, to the day. She had once celebrated his twenty-second birthday by kissing him many times, while hiding in the moonlit shrubbery at the edge of Mrs. Bentley-Morgan's velvety lawn. She recalled every detail of those precious kisses, as alive in her memory as if they had happened last night.

Eleanor turned to a safer subject. "Were your new dresses delivered?"

"Two of them, but the ball gown will never do. It is so very white it makes my face appear as yellow as a lemon."

"Let me come to your boudoir and see what the problem is." Eleanor found the Prima's docility in the weeks they had been in London to be both unusual and welcome, but little lapses were certainly to be expected.

Priscilla gestured defiantly to a frothy gown spread on her counterpane, as snowy as tradition prescribed. "Grandmother says I have to wear white, which makes me look positively sickly. I shall order it made over in pink."

Eleanor nodded, suppressing a bit of a grin. "You know your complexion best, Priscilla, but perhaps we could try a pink underskirt instead of the white slip. The sheerest white layers will take on a pinkish hue."

Priscilla frowned. "I suppose so." She reached for a fan lying next to boxes of gloves, shawls, and stockings. "And I suppose I will be expected to carry one of these silly things. I find them ridiculous. I will look as ancient as Grandmother."

"But they are so very convenient for covering a whispered conversation."

Priscilla tossed the fan toward its box. "I am quite prepared to take all of your advice, Eleanor, for I think you have better taste and far better manners than Violet—even though she managed to capture a duke in her first Season and you never made a match after several years."

Eleanor smoothed the dress and attempted to keep her voice steady. "There are other considerations in life besides marriage. I made my choice and I am satisfied." She could not, would not lose her composure and allow a trace of the truth slip out.

"You do not have to live with Violet. With her around, Father hardly ever spends any time at the Hall. She sends me on errand after errand while she is too lazy to get off her couch."

"I should not allow you to speak so of your stepmama."

"Would you rather have me tell Charlotte Sanderson all about her?"

"No, my dear, but you should try not to have such impertinent thoughts."

"I tell you, I will be glad to leave Branden forever. I must find a husband to take me away so I need never return."

"Why, Priscilla, you do not mean that!"

Priscilla nodded vigorously, setting her golden ringlets a-tumble. "Perhaps 'never' is the wrong word. But to live far away from Violet and Grandmother sounds like heaven to me."

"I shall overlook your outburst, Cousin dear, but be assured that it is my wish to help you find a match this very year. And Violet is also your ally, you know."

"She will have to find someone else to do her bidding night and day. But you are correct in thinking she will be happy to be rid of me."

"Your choice of words does you no credit, Priscilla. These are thoughts you must keep to yourself. I will not betray your confidence, but I daresay you should put these feelings aside. You must be on your best behavior today, for I am quite sure we shall have some callers this afternoon, perhaps some you will wish to impress. Pouting and sulks are never becoming to one's good looks."

Priscilla pushed the dress aside and sat down on the bed. "Do not concern yourself, Eleanor. I intend to be at my radiant best in an hour or two. I have already spied the several bouquets of flowers delivered this morning. One is from Lord Bromley."

Eleanor forced a smile. "Then I shall leave you to settle your nerves and dress. Something very modest, my dear."

Eleanor rushed back to her room and stared at her flaming cheeks in the mirror. Griff had sent flowers to the Prima?

She sank into a chair and covered her face with her hands. This was no time to indulge in tears and make her face blotchy and swollen.

Violet chose to come down that afternoon to receive callers. She ensconced herself on the settee,

pulling a shawl around her and keeping her vinaigrette close at hand. She was plumply pretty, a
vacant smile on her face. After three days of hardly
leaving her room, she claimed to be feeling better,
though Eleanor suspected the duchess was primar-
ily curious to see who might appear.

Violet arranged and rearranged her shawls. "If I
feel a chill, Eleanor, please see that Pratt adjusts the
draperies immediately. I so fear . . ."

Her words were interrupted by the arrival of
Hartselle. After performing exaggerated and obsequious courtesies to all three ladies, Hartselle
launched into a description of several eligible men
for Priscilla. His attire was as colorful and out-
landish as yesterday's, pantaloons in a startling
shade of yellow and a turquoise coat adorned with
buttons made of mother-of-pearl. Priscilla and Violet both wore brilliant shades, according to what
was claimed to be the latest mode. In her round
gown of soft blue, Eleanor felt as dull as a little wren
in a cage of canaries.

She surreptitiously looked at the cards that came
with the flowers, only half listening to Hartselle's
list until one name jumped out.

"Then there is the new Lord Bromley, who will
succeed to the earldom of Edenhurst. Fine fellow
and in need of a wife."

"A new baron?" Violet asked.

"Indeed. A terrible story."

Eleanor watched as Hartselle wiggled in joyful
anticipation of spilling juicy gossip to a new set of
ears.

"He was the younger son, you know. Some strange
relationship with the army—worked for the engineers,

technical things. His elder brother James was a bit of an irresponsible gambler, who cut a fine figure at the mills, and raced his horses at the Goodwood meet. Poor man could not resist a wager and so he met his end in a curricle race. It was said to be a dreadful scene."

Hartselle shook his head in mock mourning. "All this was more than a year ago. It is said the new Lord Bromley wants to marry soon, to comfort his dear mama."

The words had barely left his lips when Pratt announced, "Lady Edenhurst, Lord Bromley, and Mrs. Smithers."

Eleanor glanced at the last card, perched in a spray of yellow and white blossoms. It read simply, "Bromley." There was no salutation. Relieved, she took a step toward the door. Priscilla almost bounded up to the visitors and made her curtsies. Eleanor forced her fingers to relax and uncurl, avoiding Griff's eyes while greeting all three of the callers.

A little scream of delight came from Violet as she caught a glimpse of Mrs. Smithers. "Why, Harriet, my darling, how very good to see you!"

Mrs. Smithers flew to the duchess' side, and they fluttered in and out of each other's arms, both talking at once and generally causing everyone to pause and watch the tender and joyous scene.

"Apparently they are enjoying their reunion." Griff wore a look of amusement as he gazed at the two females.

Eleanor stole a glance at him.

"I think it is lovely." Lady Edenhurst dabbed at her eyes with a bit of lace.

In a few moments, they settled themselves on chairs surrounding Violet's chaise.

Lady Edenhurst, still in black, her face lined by tragedy, nevertheless presented a handsome image. Obviously Griff's good looks came in part from his mother's side of the family.

Violet dried her cheeks. "At school, Harriet was always my ideal, being a bit older."

Mrs. Smithers pressed a hand to her heart. "Oh, no, my dear, the situation is reversed. I admired you, for I always thought you were the elder."

Eleanor stifled a chuckle and turned her attention to Lady Edenhurst, who was peering intently at Priscilla. From the girl's flaxen hair to her silken slippers, Priscilla was being inspected as if the countess were purchasing an ell of silk or appraising the workmanship of a jeweled brooch. Eleanor pitied the countess, for it must have been dreadful for her to lose her cherished first son, in whom she took so much pride. Now she must be devoted to having her heritage carried on by Griff. To do so, she was clearly thinking of Priscilla as a prospective match for him—not only a young and pretty bride, but a fine alliance for her family.

Griff, his face registering no emotion, had taken a place between Hartselle and his mother.

Eleanor wished she could disappear, sink into the thick Axminster carpet, instead of witnessing the budding acquaintance of her cousin Priscilla with the man she, Eleanor, had loved secretly for the last six years.

For a moment, Eleanor turned her attention to Violet and Harriet, who were busily exchanging the names of medications for an astonishing array of

complaints. Violet's only real affliction, as far as
Eleanor could tell, was a tendency to overindulge
herself in sweets and an ability to avoid any physical
activity whatsoever. The other complaints were all a
part of her lassitude, for no one's stomach could
tolerate a steady diet of sugar without having its
sour moments.

The thought brought a smile to Eleanor's lips,
and she suddenly felt Griff's gaze on her. When
their eyes met, his were soft, his gaze as sweet as she
remembered. She might never have looked away,
but Pratt came to the door.

"The Marquess of Arlford, Viscount Peters, and
Sir Gavin Gawthorpe."

All the while Eleanor welcomed the guests, introduced them around the room, then hastened
again to receive a third set of callers, her mind spun
with possible implications of Griff's expression. She
longed for a moment to speak to him, but not in
the midst of the drawing room now teeming with
people.

The youthful Lord Peters nodded his way in, a
silly smile on his face, a young man with a long
neck well suited to the high shirt points and layers
of cravat wound around it.

His father, Lord Arlford, addressed the duchess.
"I am pleased you are in London. You have not
been here in the last few Seasons."

Violet adopted an attitude of deep suffering. "I
am sadly afflicted with so many complicated mal-
adies I find Society a strain to my poor nerves. But
of course for my darling Priscilla I will make any
sacrifice."

Eleanor almost choked and had to fight back the

temptation to ask Violet to name a single sacrifice she had made—or indeed any exertion at all on Priscilla's behalf other than her mere presence.

Violet placed her chin on the back of her hand and sighed. "I would do anything for the dear gel."

Eleanor could not help feeling like she was trapped in the middle of a theatrical troupe performing some colorful comedy for which she had forgotten all her lines. She poured and handed around a series of teacups that no one seemed to sip. Voices broke into exclamations of surprise or laughter that Eleanor could not comprehend. Instead of a play, she thought, it began to seem like a nightmare.

Again the bustle of arrivals and departures drew Eleanor from the center of the room. As she said good-bye to Lord Arlford, she stole a peek at Griff, now talking to Priscilla. Eleanor yearned to have just a moment alone with him, try to understand what he had meant by his remark about her rejection of him. She wanted to ask why he had left London so quickly, why she had never heard from him again, though how she could bring up those matters she could not imagine.

She followed Lord Arlford and Lord Peters to the top of the steps, closing the door of the drawing room behind her. When the gentlemen were gone, she leaned both hands on the cool marble surface of the pier table and took a deep, shuddering breath. Just yesterday at this hour she and the Prima had departed for the musicale in blissful ignorance of what was about to occur. Eleanor wished she could turn back the clock, join Violet in a fit of the sullens and obliterate the sight of Griffith Preston.

She looked up quickly when she heard the door open again.

Griff shut it quietly and walked to her side.

"Norrie, I wish to—"

"Could you explain—"

They spoke at once and both stopped abruptly.

He started again. "I am sure you find this as awkward as I do."

She kept her eyes down, for if she allowed herself to look at his face, she feared she would simply melt into his arms.

"Norrie, I wish I could explain or try to understand . . ."

"It was a very long time ago—"

As Pratt led them upstairs, the sound of more arrivals below cut off her words.

Eleanor rushed back to the drawing room, her cheeks burning.

When she greeted Mrs. Sanderson and Charlotte, she noticed Griff followed them into the room. Their brief encounter only made things worse.

Only as Lady Edenhurst and Mrs. Smithers made their farewells did she stand near him again. But he turned away quickly and addressed himself to Priscilla.

"One purpose of our visit is to seek your company at five for a turn about the park. My friend Mr. Bates and I are trying out a new team, and we solicit your opinions on their suitability. Of course, our invitation includes the duchess and your cousin as well."

Eleanor flinched. How lowering to be just "your

cousin" in such an instance. And Violet would never consent to being out of doors, so Eleanor would have to go along with Griff, or Lord Bromley, as she must accustom herself to calling him. Eleanor clenched her teeth to prevent an acid response, then resolutely turned her attentions to taking leave of the countess and Mrs. Smithers.

Priscilla simpered. "I would enjoy the park with you, Lord Bromley, but the duchess does not go out often; she is quite unwell, a malady of mysterious origin and quite unresponsive to treatment. That is precisely why my cousin has come along to act as a chaperon. You met her at the musicale, did you not?"

Eleanor had no choice. She would go along on the carriage ride and she would not allow her dismay to show. After all, Griff would never choose Priscilla as a bride. She was too flighty for his taste.

Yet Eleanor could not help wondering how she could pretend to know his taste after so many years.

Griff could think of no way to get out of the invitation now. He had no desire at all to sit in the barouche with Priscilla and Eleanor. He had not sorted out his feelings toward Eleanor, and she was obviously not comfortable with him. But he was stuck, stuck in a risky situation of his own creation.

"Damned awkward is what I call it," he told Bobby as they rode toward Branden House later that afternoon.

"So why did she refuse you all those years ago? And why does it still rankle?"

"I never learned the reason for her refusal. And it does not rankle."

"Oh, I see. How many times did you ask her to marry you?"

"Actually, never that. I asked her if I could speak to her father and she said no."

"There was no possibility of a misunderstanding?"

"No. We had spent a great deal of time together that Season. I was certain she was as eager for me to ask her to be my wife as I was to have her."

"So how many times did you ask?"

"Just once."

"Aha! Don't most young ladies avoid a positive answer until the third or fourth proposal?"

"I thought we knew each other exceedingly well. I thought we were perfectly suited for one another."

"So what happened when she turned down your request to see her father?"

"I took the next ship to the Peninsula."

"Without taking leave of her? You just walked out of her life?

"Yes, I suppose you could say that."

"My guess is that she expected you to come back and ask again, perhaps several times, before she assented. Instead, you disappeared."

"When you put it that way . . ."

"Yes. You played the tragic lover betrayed. No wonder you have never married since."

When they arrived at Branden House, a smiling Priscilla and a composed but cool Eleanor were assisted into the barouche. Priscilla took the seat next to Griff and Eleanor sat beside Bobby, directly facing Griff but keeping her eyes averted from him.

Griff tried not to look at Eleanor either, but it was very difficult. Several times the toes of her shoes brushed his boots.

Lady Priscilla wore periwinkle blue with a matching velvet bonnet crowned with curving ostrich feathers that occasionally tickled the side of his face. She was a delectable morsel, but he admitted to himself he far preferred Eleanor's appearance in her dark green outfit and bonnet free of feathers blowing in his face.

In the park, they merged into a stream of curricles and landaus making dawdling progress, stopping to exchange greetings every few yards.

There were the same exaggerated smiles, exuberant waves, and overly generous words that Griff remembered from his previous experiences in London.

As the carriages passed, Eleanor smiled and nodded to acquaintances, but kept her gaze resolutely away from him.

Priscilla leaned against him, the feathers almost causing him to sneeze.

"Lord Bromley, do you know that gentleman?" she asked, indicting a young man sitting between two elderly ladies.

"I believe that is Mr. Emerson with his mother, Lady Troup, and his aunt Mrs. Lessells."

"And who is that?"

"Mr. Goyer."

Griff found Priscilla an uninteresting young chit, no different from three or four others he was acquainted with, though of the higher status bound to appeal to his mother. None of them brought him any feelings near what he had once had for Eleanor. But she was so distant now he was more confused than ever.

Fortunately, Bobby kept up a steady stream of

comments on the horses and styles of equipages they passed, though it seemed that afternoon's fashionable hour might last forever.

If she were sitting anywhere but across from Griff, Eleanor would have laughed to herself at Priscilla's attempts to smile and flirt while remaining properly reticent and seemingly shy. Her struggles seemed to make her wiggle and brush up against Griff as well, and from what Eleanor could see from the corner of her eye, he was not discomfited.

What were his intentions? Could he be seriously interested in Priscilla? She seemed too young and foolish for a man like him. But the Prima looked the ideal candidate to steal any gentleman's heart, Eleanor thought with a jolt. The girl was as deliciously appetizing as an iced cake, delicate and tempting.

With her beauty and prospects for an ample dowry, Priscilla should attract a large number of admirers, Eleanor thought. Certainly this was the goal her cousin intended to achieve now they were officially going about in Society.

Eleanor was a bit surprised at the luxury of Griff's carriage and matched grays, the soft fur robes lined with cashmere. He was not only well dressed but his equipage spoke of an old and honored family with considerable resources. Before, he had been plain Mr. Preston, though she had known his father was an earl, of course. Why had he never come back to renew his suit? Weeks later she heard he had gone off to the Peninsula. Her dreams

about him for the past six years might have created
a person rather unlike what he actually was.

It seemed to her that Griff was very good at this
Society business. For a man who had once claimed
to be such an outsider, so disgusted with the nonsensical pretensions and arrogances of the *ton*, he
bore the trappings well. Either he had changed in
his outlook or he was an accomplished charlatan.
Neither role seemed possible for the man she
loved, a man who now seemed only a figment of
her imagination.

Perhaps he was no different from all the rest of
them. When they came to London every year, they
all played the same roles and engaged the same
backstage assistants. Tailors, bookmakers, hatters,
modistes, shoemakers, milliners, purveyors of
gloves, reticules, silk lingerie, carriage makers,
jewelers—all depended upon the custom of the
ton, the service of the fashionable in their pursuit
of both pleasure and enhanced status. Troupes
of dancing masters, vocal coaches, elocution and
pianoforte teachers—a legion was hired to polish the questionable abilities of young ladies being
paraded in the marriage mart. The yearly display
brought even more to Town, the deserving and
the poseurs, the imperious few at the top and
those who aspired to ascend, the scrambling near-
gentry and the money-laden cits.

They all had their roles, players in the dramas
acted out on the Season's stage.

Four

The Dowager Duchess of Branden scowled as Eleanor read her the nearly endless list of more than two hundred guests who had accepted invitations for Priscilla's ball. But at the conclusion, she pronounced herself satisfied. Her friends were included, every *arriviste* eliminated.

"I am pleased, Eleanor. You seem to have snagged the correct people."

Eleanor gave a little sigh of relief. "I am completely certain the acceptance of the first stare of the *ton* has much more to do with the Milford-Branden family than any efforts on my part."

"You are correct, but your work has done credit to our name. I have had correspondence confirming that, you know."

"I am pleased to hear it."

Eleanor fingered the pale blue hangings of the dowager's bed. Her grandmother was propped up against a dozen pillows. A plate of toast and a spirit lamp sat on the bedside table.

"Call Mason to light some pastilles, Eleanor. The air is musty in here. The room was not properly aired."

"I am sorry. I thought the housekeeper carried out her duties sufficiently."

"It is not your fault. Mrs. Arnold takes her house-keeping instructions from Violet, and when you have a ninny in charge, the help will often be as lazy and as careless as their mistress."

Eleanor delivered the message and watched Mason carry out her instructions.

The dowager straightened her lacy cap and shrugged. "I suppose you had no choice but to include that silly ass Hartselle."

"Violet is quite attached to him."

The dowager gave a snort of disgust. "That does not surprise me. He is exactly the kind of coxcomb she would favor."

"To be honest, Priscilla and I have also enjoyed his gossip. How he learns some of the things he says is very hard to imagine."

"Indeed. I find him tiresome, but, as you say, occasionally amusing in a superficial, cheeky sort of way." She took a sip of tea and made a face. "I shall need a fresh pot. This is as weak as Violet's brew."

"I will see to it immediately."

Now that the cloying scent of the pastilles wafted through the room, Eleanor welcomed the opportunity to go to the kitchen and oversee the proper preparation of the tray. Plus, the trip downstairs and back up gave her a moment's breathing room. Ever since the party from Branden Hall arrived, she hardly had a moment to call her own.

The duke had accompanied his mother and assorted sisters and cousins to town a week earlier. Eleanor was certain their entourage could have supplied several regiments of Wellington's army. The aunts bustled around Mayfair greeting their friends, acquiring new ensembles in the most fashionable styles, and keeping the servants rushing with their errands.

In one way, Eleanor valued the commotion. She had less time to dwell on her obsession with Griff. Below the surface her emotions swirled, frustrating and maddening. When in his presence, she was usually able to prevent her gaze from meeting his across the room, but she never lost her awareness of him. She had torn up more than a dozen notes she tried to write. Not a single one expressed her thoughts, probably because those thoughts changed again and again. One moment she wanted to entice him into renewing their old romance; the next, she pledged never to think of him again and go back to her school without caring what happened to him. Then there was the unendurable possibility he might marry her cousin, a possibility that ruined many nights of sleep.

Time had flown by. There was the last-minute flurry of preparations for yesterday's Queen's Drawing Room. Their Branden House ball at which Priscilla would be formally introduced to Society was scheduled for tomorrow evening. Eleanor knew she must fortify herself against the pain of watching Griff dance with Priscilla, as she strongly suspected Violet and Lady Edenhurst would arrange it.

When Eleanor reached the lower level, Pratt was beside himself. "Miss Milford, you need not come down yourself. One of the footmen could have come. I trust that Cutter was in his proper station."

"Of course he was. I merely wished to be certain the tea caddy is sent up."

"Of course."

Cook grinned and waved a hand at her busy

cadre of helpers already preparing sweets for the midnight supper. "We'r doin' the preparations, you tell 'er Grace. No finer lobster puffs 'n England than mine."

"Nor do your tarts have an equal in all the realm."

Eleanor preceded Pratt up the two flights. The sound of pounding came from the ballroom as the footmen prepared to hang the pink and white striped silk she had chosen. At the last moment, the walls would be embellished with cascades of ivy and blush roses. She imagined the effect would be stunning against the mirrored walls and gilt trim.

At her grandmother's side, Eleanor settled into her chair, grateful that the odor of the pastilles was less obvious. Pratt set the tray before the dowager and arranged a heavy linen napkin around the handle of the steaming pot of water.

"Thank you, Pratt."

Grandmother, Eleanor thought, had precisely the right tone of appreciation in those three words, uttered with the exact degree of condescension to satisfy the exacting standards of a fastidious butler such as Pratt. He bowed his way out, a slight smile on his lips.

Eleanor watched the dowager duchess generously measure the tea. "I have asked several gentlemen to dance with Priscilla. She must be the center of attention at the ball, never without a partner. I hope that meets with your approval."

"I don't suppose Violet has lifted a finger to help."

Eleanor could not resist smiling. "As you say, Grandmother."

"Give me a list of these eligible men."

"Lord Peters, Sir Gavin . . ." She named several more. "Lord Bromley."

"Bromley? He is a dedicated gambler. Steer clear of him."

"No." Eleanor tried to sound unconcerned. "The poor man was killed in an accident. This is a new Lord Bromley, a younger brother."

"Ah!"

Eleanor quickly mentioned another pair of gentlemen.

"And what about you?"

The dowager's sudden bark startled Eleanor. "Me, grandmother? Why, I am fine. And I have not forgotten our bargain."

"Nor have I! If you get that chit betrothed, you can have your school. But I want to know what happened to some of those young men who adored you a few Seasons ago. All married to someone else? Or cannon fodder?"

Startled, Eleanor did not know if her shudder was for the topic or the bluntness of the duchess's language. She squirmed in her seat. Had she ever mentioned Griffith Preston to the dowager duchess? Or had the sharp-eyed old lady remembered her preference for him?

She tried to make her voice light and treat the subject as trifling. "I have no idea. Many of the faces seem quite new to me."

The dowager's left eyebrow rose as though she were perplexed. "Do not attempt to gammon me, Eleanor."

"I shall not." Eleanor quickly grabbed the list and excused herself before her wily grandmother trapped her into revealing her conundrum over Griff.

Eleanor forced the sourness in her stomach from her mind as she stood in the shadows watching the duke and duchess, the dowager duchess, and Lady Priscilla greet the handsomely attired guests at the entrance to the ballroom. She must let nothing interfere with the success of this grand ball. Nothing!

So far, the servants, with many extras hired for the evening, seemed to be coping with the requests and eccentricities of the guests. With the dowager in attendance, her old friends had arrived, many of them infirm and needful of assistance to convey their carcasses upstairs. Anticipating just such a situation, Eleanor had hired two of the sturdiest dockhands Pratt could secure. Cleaned up and suited in the Branden livery, much remodeled to accommodate their sturdy forms, they had managed to assist a number of elderly aristocrats, including Lady Simondson, whose rotund form bulged from a gown large enough to tent the entire area of Berkeley Square. As long as the fellows kept their mouths shut, their epithets to themselves, and their opinions on the oddity of carrying old nobs upstairs saved, all was well.

The kitchen staff had turned out a creditable dinner for the family, at least eighteen people around the large table, with three removes of the dowager's preferred veal cutlets, the duke's favorite mutton, Violet's ideal turbot, and everyone's favorite dishes, as many as Eleanor could recall. The musicians were as expert as their reputations had promised. The preparations for a midnight supper were complete.

As the dancing got under way, Aunt Sophy tapped Eleanor's shoulder. For the last three days, Sophy had tried, hoped, yearned to find a tiny chore left undone, a dish imperfectly prepared, or a decoration out of place. Eleanor had listened to her list of problems without flinching, and now prepared to hear of a detail overlooked.

"My dear Eleanor, you have accomplished perfection. Though I do find the pale pinks a tiny bit anemic. A slightly deeper hue might have been a little livelier, do you not agree?"

"Undoubtedly so, Aunt Sophy."

"And I detect a bit too much pink in Priscilla's gown. But I suppose you could not convince her that a pure white would be more proper and above reproach?"

The fortunate arrival of Mrs. Ottway, Sophy's dearest friend, allowed Eleanor to swallow her temptation to deliver her opinion of Aunt Sophy's puce satin ensemble, complete with towering and tastelessly bejeweled turban. While Sophy effused over Mrs. Ottway, Eleanor excused herself and hurried away, intent to go as far away from her aunt as she could.

She almost bumped into Lady Edenhurst, who grasped her wrist and drew Eleanor into a conversation with Mrs. Smithers.

"How lovely Lady Priscilla looks, my dear. And such a sweet child, an angel. According to her, you are to be credited with her polish."

Eleanor demurred. "Not at all. I am merely here to accompany her when the duchess is indisposed."

To herself, Eleanor wondered if Lady Edenhurst could ever envisage the Prima's usual impudent behavior or the amount of instruction it had taken to convert her into the angel who so enchanted everyone.

"She is a credit to her stepmother." Mrs. Smithers gazed at the crowd as if seeking Violet in the midst of the dancers, a situation Eleanor found almost comical. Only this afternoon they had to beg Violet not to insist on placing her chaise in the middle of the ballroom so that she could recline while watching the dancers. For once the duke had asserted his authority.

As the dance set came to a conclusion, Eleanor felt in jeopardy standing with Lady Edenhurst and Harriet, as though she were trying to waylay Griff. Lord Bromley, she reminded herself for the hundredth time.

"If you will excuse me, I should attend to my Grandmother again." She hurried around the edges of the room and found the dowager duchess chatting away with a group of friends who somehow reminded Eleanor of the Cruikshank drawing of the Pump Room at Bath thirty years ago.

Most of them wore clothing more suited to that time, including more than one powdered wig and several out-of-fashion gowns with panniers in the style of the King's daughters' outdated court apparel. But they were all as animated as could be, brandishing their fans, waving lace-cuffed hands, and lifting their quizzing glasses to survey the room. It was obvious the dowager would not relish interruption, so Eleanor faded back into the potted palms and drew a deep breath. Every detail was under control. Except one. She simply must avoid any contact with Griff. She dared not risk someone noticing a look between them that spoke volumes about their past.

Hartselle materialized beside her. "You must come and dance with me, Eleanor. All the family is on the floor."

Eleanor could not help feeling that danger lurked in every corner of this crowded ballroom. Not only were there a thousand little things that could go awry, from dripping candles to spilled punch, there were assorted guests who might not deign to speak to someone else's cousin, or someone who had too much wine might take offense at another's innocent remark. Priscilla might fall into her old impetuous ways and do something foolish while everyone watched. Not only did all these and more disasters threaten, she was sure to see Griff if she danced.

But she could not think of any reasonable excuse to decline Hartselle's unexpected request, and followed him to the country dance forming up in the center of the room.

Her nerve almost failed when she saw Griff lead Priscilla into the set. *Take hold of yourself. You have been doing these dances since childhood. Why would you stumble now?*

The music began, and like a sleepwalker she curtsied and skipped through the steps, repetition after repetition. When they came to the inevitable pairing with Priscilla and Griff, she forced a smile and tried to suppress the tingle she felt on each crossover when her fingers touched his.

The touch of no one else caused her the slightest unease, and yet she wanted to take his hand and not let go. *Fool! For too many years you have let these old romantic notions flit about in your silly head!*

When the sets re-formed, she grabbed Hartselle's hand and dragged him away.

"I am parched, Cousin. Can we find the refreshments?"

"Even better." Hartselle plucked two glasses of champagne from the tray of a passing waiter.

Eleanor took a deep swallow, then another, though she knew she should not. She needed to keep her head. Eventually she could drive away her old emotions, but for tonight, she must avoid being near Griff, hearing him speak, feeling his touch.

As Hartselle launched into pithy comments on the gown worn by Cousin Olivia, Eleanor looked back at the dancers. She could stay distant from Griff, perhaps, but she probably could not cease her admiration for his long legs and broad shoulders, his masculine grace.

She wished she could simply leave the ball and go upstairs to her room, crawl under the covers, and compose a letter to Jane.

But she had to stay here. She had no choice.

Griff stood behind a screen of elderly gentlemen discussing when to retire to the card room. He had performed his obligatory dance with the belle of the hour, Lady Priscilla. Afterward she chattered, hardly taking a breath, while he waited with her for a passing waiter to bring a cool beverage. He was relieved when Lord Peters claimed her. At least his mother would be satisfied.

He looked around the crowded salon, unconsciously carried back six years to a party much like this when, as it came to a close, he asked Eleanor if he could speak to her father and she refused. He had been much younger, no prospects for a fortune, no prospects whatsoever.

Before that awful ending, he hardly had been able to refrain from audible sighs at the vision of Norrie, glowing in an ivory gown, gilded roses in her hair. He was captivated, the luckiest man in London. They danced, promenaded through brightly lit rooms, laughed over plates of food they barely touched. He could not remember what they spoke of or why their eyes had remained locked together for so long. Then the unexpected setback. The painful blow.

He must know why. He needed to know, and tonight was the time to ask her. No one was paying any attention to him. He had to attempt to talk to her.

He strolled around the room, trying to look at ease. When he saw her, he approached from the side and managed to catch her attention without interrupting the gathering's conversation. Though she looked surprised to see him, he moved closer and bent toward her ear.

"Please meet me at the stairs in a quarter hour."

Her eyes wide as if in fright, she stared at him for an instant, gave a quick nod, and turned away. Fifteen minutes later, he waited near the door of the ballroom, hoping she would honor her quick acquiescence.

He fingered his watch, but did not bother to open it.

She stepped out of the room, glancing behind her almost furtively.

"Norrie? Is there someplace we can talk?"

She did not meet his eyes. "I cannot be gone but a moment."

"I understand. But I feel we must clarify . . ."

She spoke quickly, nervously. "Yes, yes. Follow me."

When he closed the door of the library behind them, he wasted no time. "I find our situation as awkward as you must find it. Some months ago, I assured my mother she would have a major role in choosing my wife this Season. You see . . ."

"Yes, and she has intimated to me that she favors my cousin, Lady Priscilla."

"Let me start again. I apologize if this question is upsetting to you, Norrie, but I have always been curious. Why did you turn down my suit?"

Her surprise at this turn of the conversation showed clearly on her face. "I have asked myself the very same question. You see, the truth is there was no reason at all. It was a frivolous decision for me, actually no decision at all."

"You mean, you simply did not care about me?"

"No!" She spoke quickly. "Quite the contrary. I was very fond of you."

He nodded, his long-held opinion confirmed. "I thought we were very compatible at the time."

"As did I. I was young and foolish, in no hurry to set up a household."

"You wanted something else from life?"

"No, not a different life from what was expected of me. I liked living at our little house on the Branden estate. I loved being spoiled by my mother and father. I enjoyed all of life."

"I know you did. That was your most engaging

quality, your interest in everything, however great or small."

"If I had known how fragile that life was, I might have reacted differently."

"What do you mean?"

"Only a few months later, in the autumn of 1811, my mother took ill. She was in great pain for a long time, very sad and very difficult. My father was heartsick. We all were helpless to ease her suffering. By the time she died a year later, I had become a quite different person."

"I am sorry to hear of your difficulties. You must have anguished, too."

"Thank you. Griff, I am sorry we parted without talking over the reasons for my reply to you. I was foolish, frivolous, a silly chit indeed. I assure you I did not mean to drive you away. I did not choose my words carefully. I blurted out the words in a hurtful manner, I am sure."

He stood motionless, trying to absorb her meaning.

"Your mother and father did not approve of me."

"Their opinions meant nothing."

"If I had stayed in London, you would have seen me again?"

Suddenly her calm demeanor broke and, with a sob, she covered her face with her hands. "I wanted nothing more."

He pulled her into his arms. "Norrie?"

She took a shuddering breath and pushed him away. "I must go. I will be missed."

"But—"

He stopped speaking as she pulled open the door and fled.

He let his empty arms drop to his sides. Deuce take it, the entire mess was his fault, the blunder of a proud and stubborn fool, afraid to risk a second rejection.

Griff let his anger boil up again, anger at himself, not her. Somehow the thoughtless nature of her action was worse than if she had said she was in love with someone else or wanted a man with a title and position. Of all the reasons he had pondered, he never guessed she might not have meant her answer. He thought she had a reason. Now it appeared there was none.

He forced himself to take a deep breath and stop pacing. So he had the answer to one question, but now he needed to know more, much more. Did she understand why he had left, that he had loved her? Or that he still loved her?

Would Norrie be amenable to renewing their friendship and seeing where it led?

He had to find a way to ask her before his mother and the duchess had him irretrievably tied to Norrie's cousin. Priscilla might make someone a biddable wife. More likely she would make someone miserable.

The situation was ticklish, to say the least. He must continue to pay calls at Branden House. Everyone would assume he was courting Priscilla. But otherwise, how could he see Norrie and somehow learn if she could care for him again?

Five

The presence of the entire family at Branden House meant Eleanor could avoid social calls and airings in the park for several days following the presentation ball. She tried to stay alone in her room as much as possible, for she had no taste for rehashing the events of the ball over and over, nor did she share enthusiasm for the many floral tributes filling the mansion with their mawkish sweet aroma.

For hours, Eleanor sat at the window of her bedchamber, staring out over the garden and the roofs of their neighbors. What had Griff said the night of the ball? Her anxiety spoiled her recollection of their talk. She knew she had told him about the pointlessness of her refusal. But what else had she said? And why had he wanted to talk at all? Perhaps he had been trying to ease her into the knowledge that he wished to offer for Priscilla.

Several more sheets of her writing paper had been torn to shreds when she could not phrase a note to him.

He had called at Branden House, once with his mother, another time alone. At neither occasion had she been present. She had to avoid him, for every time they had spoken, matters got worse.

But now the entire family discussed Lord Bromley's interest in Priscilla over breakfast and dinner.
Eleanor wondered if she should come to terms with
the thought of Griff marrying Priscilla, as dreadful
as it seemed.

By the end of the week, most of the family would
depart, and soon Jane would arrive. At last Norrie
would be able to turn her thoughts to the important reasons for being in London.

The Branden House drawing room seemed ex-
ceptionally crowded to Griff when he called a few
days after Lady Priscilla's presentation ball. But as
he made his bows to all of the ladies, he did not see
Norrie among her many aunts and cousins.

"I am your servant, Duchess." He bent low before
the dowager.

"Come sit with me, Bromley, for a moment." She
was dressed in her usual black.

Griff moved his chair closer to her. "Your family
does you credit, Your Grace."

"Like all families, we have those with accomplishments and also our share of shirkers."

He grinned, knowing she expected it.

She went on, a twinkle in her eye. "My granddaughters are the best of the lot. My great-
grand-children are just babies. Too soon to ap-
praise their value to the name. We shall see."

Griff started to speak, but she went on without a
breath.

"Now, look here, Bromley, I have passed along
my condolences to your mama on the death of your

brother. She ain't one to equivocate. Says she wants you to offer for Priscilla."

"Ah, is that what she says?" He could hardly picture the countess discussing such a subject with her. Perhaps he had underestimated the depth of his mother's resolve.

"Priscilla needs a strong hand. Impulsive gel. May be a jewel for the right fellow. But don't you be hoodwinked by her pretty face. Talk to Eleanor, her cousin. She knows."

Griff hardly knew how to respond. "I do not see Miss Milford here."

"She said she preferred to stay upstairs today. Don't like all this yapping. Nor do I. But I will take most of these chattering magpies with me when I leave tomorrow."

A tall, thin lady with graying hair curtsied to the dowager duchess. "Mother, dear, I have a little question."

Griff stood and offered his chair to the lady, whose name he did not recall. As he stepped out of the way, the dowager pointed a long finger at him.

"You speak with Eleanor. She knows what is what!"

"Thank you, Your Grace." Bowing again, he backed away. What in blazes did the duchess mean?

For the remainder of his visit, he articulated the usual pleasantries while deep in his head the questions kept eating at him. Since the ball, he had examined and reexamined Norrie's reaction to their brief conversation. He accepted her explanation, that her answer to his offer had been frivolous. He blamed his own impulsive rush from humiliation for the real ending of their romance.

But Norrie had fled the room before he could ask her to forgive, before he could ask her if there was any hope they might try again.

Now here was the dowager pushing him at Lady Priscilla just as his mother and the duchess were doing. Or did the dowager have another motive for sending him to Eleanor?

Eleanor set her teacup down and smiled at her friend. "Jane, I cannot tell you what a delight it is to have you here. Tell me everything that has happened at Branden since I left. How is Emmy coming with her letters?"

"I hated to leave them." Jane gave a little shrug. "But I am so excited to be in London. I have never seen so many people in the streets. All the traffic and noise. The horses and all sorts of equipages . . ."

Eleanor laughed out loud. "Slow down, slow down. You have weeks to see everything. How is Will?"

"Very pleased that we will look for a school for him. I left him in charge of finishing the mathematics books for the Sanders boys and little Ned." Jane lowered her voice and leaned toward Eleanor. "I am bursting to hear about Lady Priscilla. Is the Prima making an impact on the London scene?"

"To tell the truth, she is doing much better than I dared hope. She is eager to leave Violet and the duke as soon as she can. She is quite serious about finding a match, and she wants to know every detail about every gentleman she meets."

Jane's eyes twinkled. "Particularly the size of their purses? Are any of those gentlemen interested in getting to know her better?"

"Indeed they are. You will find our drawing room quite crowded with callers on the days we are at home. And why not? Most of them see only a young chit with handsome dowry prospects, good connections, and reasonable manners." An ideal description of what Griff saw, Eleanor thought with a pang.

"Then your instructions must have done wonders. I did not think she knew a whit about good behavior."

"Not my instructions but her own ambition keeps the Prima behaving herself. I doubt she is really any more measured in her behavior underneath the façade of sweet young innocence. Once she is safely attached, her old habits will be right back to spoil her reputation."

"I am glad to hear it. I would hate to think I had been so in error about her true character."

Eleanor sighed. "You are not in error, sad to say. But for the past few weeks her behavior has been exemplary, and I feel sure it will stay that way for the rest of the Season. It is not only that many of the eligible young men have very high standards. Quite a few of them are accompanied by one or both of their parents, you know."

"How interesting. I realize the young ladies need guidance and chaperonage, but I never thought the same might be true of the gentlemen."

Eleanor let that line of discussion drop. She was determined not to talk about Griff. "Where should we make inquiries about Will's future?"

For a few moments, they talked of their young protégé. Then Jane placed her hand on Eleanor's. "How are you coping with the Season, Norrie? Are you enjoying yourself?"

"Not particularly. But it will be much easier from now on, with the Queen's Drawing Room presentation and Priscilla's ball finished. I am looking forward to showing you the sights. Tonight the Prima and I go to Almack's, but tomorrow night we will take you along to Lady Brewster's rout."

"Oh, I could not!"

"Then you can turn right around and go home, Miss Wilson. I promised you could accompany us to some of the *ton*'s affairs. Who knows? You might find the man of your dreams."

"What about you, Norrie? Have you found the man of your dreams?"

Abruptly Eleanor's throat tightened and tears welled up into her eyes. She fought off the urge to confess everything. "Not at all. No, indeed." She stood and walked to the window. "It looks to be fair out of doors today. Perhaps we will take a ride in the park this afternoon."

"Norrie?" Jane pronounced the word with at least seven syllables.

The tears threatened to spill onto Eleanor's cheeks. If she dabbed at them with a hankie, Jane would not be misled. Eleanor tried to laugh, instead sounding more like a cackling goose.

Jane seemed aware of her disquiet. Eleanor fought for composure, a battle she seemed destined to reenact several times a day of late.

Spring sunshine brought teeming crowds to the city streets, and reinforced Griff's feeling of confidence. He and Bobby strolled up Bond Street and turned on Bruton toward Berkeley Square.

When they entered the square, Griff put his hand on Bobby's arm and paused. "Just wait here a moment."

"What is wrong?"

"Nothing. But see that fellow just coming down the steps of Branden House? I would rather not have to exchange pleasantries with him."

"Who is he?"

"Clarence, Lord Blythe, with whom I had a contretemps in Spain. A rotten scoundrel, in my opinion, but these days he claims to have come into a title and a fortune. I wonder, though he has ingratiated himself with enough hostesses here in town to be received almost everywhere. Though he should not be!"

"Why? What did he do?"

"I will tell you later. I hope he has not singled out Lady Priscilla for his attentions."

"Or your Miss Milford?"

"She is not my Miss Milford anymore. I have not seen her in a week, though I have called at Branden House more than once."

"I still do not understand. Are you seriously contemplating an offer of marriage to Lady Priscilla?"

"I do not know. Mother is eager for me to make that decision."

Bobby's face twisted into a scowl and his voice dripped with scorn. "Are you mad? When you love Norrie?"

"That should have been over years ago. She ran away when I tried to talk with her."

"But you could not bear to marry her cousin, could you?"

Griff shrugged. "I will live at Edenhurst, fifty miles

southwest of London. Norrie lives in Hertfordshire, thirty miles north of London. We would never meet."

"Only at every family wedding, funeral, and christening. At Christmas and Eastertide, for harvest festivals, and all through the Season in London."

"I am not concerned with London. I would be busy at home, and Norrie has a school. She is devoted to Branden."

"Use your brainbox, man. You haven't got enough sense to wear a hat in a cloudburst. What about when she tires of the school, when her father dies, or she decides to marry? She is a beautiful woman . . ."

"Stubble it, Bobby. No one denies her beauty. I simply do not know her mind on the matter."

"But your eyes go all dreamy and your voice drops down to a lovesick softness when you talk about her."

"If she condescends to appear today, I will prove I can sit in the same room and completely ignore her presence. Will that satisfy you?"

Bobby shook his head in consternation. "I will bet five guineas your face gives you away."

"That is a wager I shall win!" Griff watched Lord Blythe saunter off in the opposite direction. "We can walk on now."

The Branden House butler opened the door and bowed to Griff.

"Good afternoon, Lord Bromley."

"Good afternoon, Pratt. This is my friend Mr. Robert Bates. I hope the ladies are receiving?"

Pratt nodded to Bobby. "Indeed they are. I will take you up immediately."

When Pratt and announced them, Lady Priscilla stood and gestured to them to her side. "As you can see, Hartselle is telling Violet an ancient story about the Prince and Mrs. What's-her-name, for about the fiftieth time. So I am particularly delighted to see you."

A quick survey of the room surprised Griff. Norrie and another lady, a stranger, sat near the windows.

Griff and Bobby made their bows. "We will join you in just a moment, but I wish to say hello to the duchess and your cousin."

"Of course. But you come right back to me before Violet drags me into that nonsense again. Who cares about fat old Prinny anyway?"

Griff performed the usual courtesies for the duchess and Hartselle, making Bobby known to them. When at last he approached Norrie, she stood and looked at him, her face completely expressionless.

"Jane, may I introduce Lord Bromley and Mr. Bates? My friend Miss Jane Wilson has joined me for a visit."

Jane dropped a little curtsy.

Griff and Bobby made their bows.

"Please sit with us, gentlemen," Norrie said, her voice holding no welcome whatsoever.

Bobby immediately sat beside her.

"I promised Lady Priscilla . . ." Griff began.

Norrie's quick smile had a spurious tinge. "Oh, go to her, by all means."

"I will rejoin you later." Griff gave Bobby a look he hoped said, "I told you so."

Lady Priscilla looked as fresh and sweet and smiling as any man could wish, an eternity away from the empty glare he had received from Norrie.

Griff smiled and tried to think of a suitable topic of conversation.

Priscilla never had a shortage of subjects. "Do you take your custom to Weston, or do you have another tailor, Lord Bromley? Lord Blythe told me that Weston is the only tailor men of fashion patronize."

From his seat beside Lady Priscilla, he could not help watching an animated conversation among Norrie, Bobby, and Miss Wilson, but he tried to attend to Priscilla's words, however trivial. "As a matter of fact, Lady Priscilla, I did acquire this coat from Weston, but I assure you there are many others in London who can turn out a gentleman in fine style. I believe it was Brummell and his friends who made Weston a name."

"Did you know Mr. Brummell?"

"I never had the privilege of making his acquaintance." Griff found himself trying to listen to the conversation on the other side of the room instead of concentrating on Lady Priscilla.

"I wish he was still in London, for I have heard he had a soft spot for certain young ladies."

"Surely you do not need any assistance in charming the entire *ton,* Lady Priscilla." His own obsequiousness left a bad taste in his mouth. He could hear Bobby laughing and Norrie, too. He wondered what they were talking about.

"Of course even now, Lord Bromley, it is said there are persons whose attention can bring a young lady to the forefront of Society, just by speaking to her in the right places."

"My, such power in just talking with a person?"

"You do not believe such men exist?"

He heard the evocative sound of Norrie's laughter, and his innards twisted as with pain.

Lady Priscilla did not seem to notice his inattention. "You might be such a person yourself, Lord Bromley."

As he was about to reply and deny the possibility, Pratt opened the drawing room door.

"Lord Peters."

Lady Priscilla turned and watched the gawky young man stop to give his regards to the duchess, then walk to her side.

Griff stood and acknowledged the viscount, then gestured to his seat beside Lady Priscilla. "Please, take my place for the moment. Lady Priscilla, your servant." Griff gave a little bow and turned to join Bobby, Norrie, and Miss Wilson near the windows.

As Griff took his seat, Bobby slapped his knee and grinned. "These two ladies will soon be leading the parade, Griff. They have themselves a fine little school."

Griff nodded, recalling he had heard Norrie say she was some sort of teacher.

Bobby went on. "And they have a pupil I think I might like to have in my program in a year or two."

Norrie's face lit up with enthusiasm. "Do you think he could be a mapmaker? He has a true aptitude for mathematics and strong curiosity about geography."

Abruptly she looked at Griff, halted her comments, and again assumed a chilly mask.

Griff wondered why she talked to Miss Wilson and to Bobby but when she remembered his presence, she froze up. Was she angry with him? Or upset about his supposed attentions to her cousin?

He looked at her again, and felt a rush of emotion. If she gave him the tiniest bit of encouragement, he would offer her everything. Her eyes met his for an instant. Did he see a matching feeling there, something like the love he once believed in, then lost? Did it blossom again?

She looked away quickly and he turned also, meeting this time the full gaze of Bobby, who gave a knowing grin and a bit of a nod. Griff had not won his wager. Not by a long shot, and Bobby saw it clearly.

Eleanor stared at her hands, willing them to be still and protect her veneer of calm. Inside she struggled to ignore Griff and conceal her feeling from Jane, whose sharp gaze she felt from time to time.

She found the conversation far too interesting, even exciting, to hear Bobby tell about how he and Griff had mapped battlefields in the Peninsula. This was not helping her destroy her feelings for Griff, as she had pledged to do.

Jane, however, had no reticence about asking every question that occurred to her. "So after you served in Portugal and Spain, you came back to England?"

Bobby nodded. "We did, except for that little detour to Belgium."

Eleanor gasped. "You were at the Battle of Waterloo?"

"Not far away. We were mapping the terrain nearby with the engineers, but when things heated up, we who carried no weapons had to retreat from the action."

"No weapons but our surveying tools, which are not of much help once the shooting starts."

Jane sat back in her chair and looked perplexed. "I cannot imagine being on the battlefield at all, but especially without guns or swords."

Griff took up the story. "Back here in England we both joined up with the trigonometric mapping project of the entire kingdom."

Eleanor could not resist a question, but she directed it to Mr. Bates.

"What is the trigonometric survey?"

Griff answered. "We worked for the survey after we returned from Belgium until Bobby went off to teach more surveyors and I had the bad luck to . . ." His voice faded away, and Eleanor stole a look at his face. He stared off, as if into the distance, and he looked troubled.

Bobby cuffed him on the shoulder. "Aw, Griff, you know if you try you can do more than anyone with that land. And map every blade of grass and grasshopper hideout while you are at it. Do not burden the young ladies with your regrets, Griff. You may have mapped six counties or more, but you will be just as good a steward of the land as you are a surveyor."

Griff brought a smile to his lips, if not quite to his entire countenance. "I am reasonably sure Bobby overstates my abilities, but I shall try."

Jane voiced Eleanor's thought. "Please, tell us more about that survey. What did you call it?"

Griff addressed both of them. "The trigonometical survey? It is very simple, a form of measurement based on triangles. We measure the distance between two landmarks, say a church steeple and a capstone of a bridge. When we have that measurement, we find a third point, another unchanging landmark. From each end of the original line, we measure the angles of lines to their meeting at a third point. The size of the angles gives us the information to calculate the distance, a matter of basic trigonometry."

Eleanor looked at Jane. "I think I understand. You are better at mathematics than I am, Jane. Do you understand?"

"I think so."

Bobby took out a piece of paper and demonstrated the process. "When you have a perfectly measured triangle, you use each side to begin the next triangles. Soon you have covered an area with a series of triangles, showing the distances between exact points on the land."

Griff added to the explanation. "You will be amazed to see how accurate and precise these triangles are."

Eleanor noticed Lord Peters standing and making his good-byes to Priscilla. Jane seemed on the verge of asking more questions when Lord Peters came to briefly pay his respects on his way out. Griff and Mr. Bates added their good-byes and left on the heels of Lord Peters.

Eleanor almost sighed with relief. However fascinated she was with Griff and Bobby's conversation, she needed to be away from Griff's troubling presence. She felt as though she rode a seesaw up and down, her emotions raw and bruised, her head spinning with contradictory thoughts.

She sat here spellbound by the man. But he was a man she really did not know at all, a man who existed largely in her own imagination. In reality, a man who did not fit her future. She knew what she wanted to do: educate children.

Had she not made that decision and given up her once held wish for marriage and motherhood? Why was she allowing the possibility of reconsideration?

She must have been saying the proper things, for soon the drawing room was empty of guests, except for Hartselle, who still sat at Violet's side.

Eleanor stood. "Jane, I feel the need for an invigorating turn about the square. Will you accompany me?"

"A walk will be just the thing." Jane lowered her voice to a whisper. "And, Norrie, while we are walking, I want you tell me all about your reunion with Lord Bromley."

"What?" Eleanor was sure she had not given away her tangle of emotions regarding Griff this afternoon.

"I strongly suspect you are about to make another serious mistake."

Eleanor hurried to her bedchamber, ostensibly to change into a dress and shoes suitable for walking. She badly needed to recover her sensibilities. This was only the second day of Jane's visit, and already her friend had figured out the essence of her situation.

What could she do? Continue to deny? Had Jane not already seen enough to make that useless? She could admit everything and ask Jane to help her put the romance, her mistake, and Griff behind her.

If she followed that path, she would still have to deal with the fact that Griff seemed to have some interest in Priscilla, a situation over which Eleanor had no control. But it was surely necessary for her to learn to live with the potential of Griff's presence in the family.

Of course there was another path, one that she had hardly dared think, much less put into words for Jane. Even so, Jane might think of the possibility herself, the possibility that Eleanor insistently refused to consider, the possibility that Griff might still care for her, the possibility she might reverse her mistake. *But no, it is impossible. Too many obstacles stand in the way.*

Eleanor examined her face in the mirror, somehow amazed that she looked almost normal when her mind was in such a whirl. Her cheeks were not as pink as Jane's, her eyes less bright as well. Jane was much more animated than usual.

Of course! The attentions of Mr. Bates had centered on Jane, and Jane loved it.

Eleanor smiled as she changed her shoes to sturdy half boots. *Now, Miss Jane Wilson, our conversation will take a different turn!*

Jane practically leaped down the steps to the pavement. "I never realized how I would miss being out of doors. I have a new appreciation of nature. Except that here, instead of the lowing of the cows and the crow of the rooster, we hear the rumble of a hundred carriages and wagons."

Eleanor took Jane's arm and they began to stroll. "You have not yet experienced Hyde Park. It is the most beautiful in the city and has rolling hills, the Serpentine, and carriage paths everywhere. As beautiful a verdure as you have ever seen."

"The attractions of the city are many indeed, but for beauty's sake, I doubt the countryside will ever be improved upon."

"Jane, I will no longer argue my case, for we are both right in our way. Some of the noble architecture, such as the portico of Carlton House or the dome of St. Paul's Cathedral would make a good case on my side, but until you have experienced them, I cannot expect you to understand."

"Oh ho, Norrie, my friend, I must bow to your very superior knowledge."

"As you shall soon know, a temporary condition."

They turned the corner and traversed the pavement before the northern row of houses.

Jane tightened her grip on Eleanor's arm. "Tell me about Lord Bromley."

"He is a dear friend of Mr. Bates, who seemed to have taken quite a fancy to you."

"I admit I find him rather appealing. But I am certain he has a wife and a passel of children at home."

"On the contrary. I happen to know he is a bachelor."

Jane gave a little smile. "Probably one of those bachelors who is charming but feckless."

"But if he were to become interested . . ."

"Norrie, we are supposed to be talking about you and Lord Bromley."

"I never agreed to that exclusive topic, you know."

Raindrops began to splatter on their bonnets. The sky had darkened, and they hurried back to the house.

As they gained the protection of the foyer, Eleanor shook out her skirts. "If only we had carried our umbrellas, the rain would have stayed far away."

"That is always true."

"Pratt, would you please light the fire in the library? We should like to have tea there."

"Very good, Miss Milford."

In a quarter hour, Jane and Eleanor had dried themselves in front of the library fireplace and settled into the deep chairs.

Jane looked at the rows of bookshelves. "This is a lovely room, friendly and cozy. The rest of the house is more like Branden Hall, huge, cavernous, and, if you don't mind my saying so, quite uncomfortably drafty."

"I wholeheartedly agree."

"Now, Norrie, I have allowed you to divert me from my purpose. You may tease me all you want about Mr. Bates, but I want you to tell me about Lord Bromley. Your face when he came into the drawing room door spoke a volume."

Eleanor bristled. "Nonsense."

"You kept your eye on him every minute he was in the room."

"I most certainly did not! I listened to Mr. Bates and to you, Jane."

"All teachers develop amazing vision from the corner of their eyes. Do not pretend you have not developed the ability in our own classroom."

"As Priscilla's chaperon, it is necessary for me to keep track of what happens in that very large room."

"As I said. But I noticed particularly that when he sat down with us, your look was one of helpless adoration for a moment until you gained control of your expression, turning your countenance to stone! The extremes were quite telling!"

"Jane, your imagination is growing legendary. How can you make up such nonsense? You were gazing at Mr. Bates with an expression that said, 'Over the moon, I am over the moon!'"

"Pooh. I was trying to be polite, while you were trying to look as stern as your grandmother."

Eleanor decided her best defense was laughter. "I can hardly believe we heard a word the gentlemen were saying, so intently were we assessing each other's reactions."

Jane too broke into giggles. "Yes, indeed. But tell me the truth, Norrie. Lord Bromley is indeed the fellow you have yearned for, the one you mistakenly turned down when he suggested a more serious turn to your acquaintance?"

Eleanor sighed. "He is."

"And he is courting Priscilla?"

"It happened accidentally. A friend who did not know of our past, ah, friendship introduced him to Priscilla as prospect for her hand."

"Oh, dear."

Eleanor leaned her head back against the top of her chair. "His mother and his cousin, who is a school friend of Violet's, and the duchess are encouraging the potential match."

"But you cannot allow it!"

"How can I prevent it?"

"Eleanor, you must warn him off immediately." Jane rose and began to examine the bookshelves.

"Perhaps I should." Try as she might, Eleanor could not begin to envisage such a scene.

"Someone was a prodigious collector of books."

Eleanor was relieved to have the subject changed. "My grandfather and his forebears, too. Some of these volumes are several centuries old." She walked over and ran her hand along the spines of the books on a shelf near the large globe. She stopped and peered at one volume. "Why, here is an old atlas."

She removed the book and opened it to the title page. *"Theatre of the Empire of Great Britaine.* Jane, the date is 1612. Maps drawn by John Speed."

Jane peered over Eleanor's shoulder. "That was in the reign of James I. Imagine that!"

For several moments they carefully turned the pages of the atlas.

"It is beautiful, Norrie. And it must be quite valuable."

"Yes. I wonder if Griff, ah, Lord Bromley and Mr. Bates would want to see it?"

"I am certain they would."

Eleanor replaced the atlas on the shelf. "We will ask them next time they call."

Jane's wide grin gave her away.

"And you are hoping that will be very soon, eh, Jane?"

"You are masterful at finding ways to reroute our discussion. I have not asked you the essential question, and you have not volunteered the answer. Norrie, if Lord Bromley renewed his offer for you, would you accept?"

Eleanor clamped her lips closed on the positive reply she almost cried out. "He is no longer interested in me. He is courting the Prima."

"I find that hard to believe. I thought I saw something in the way he looked at you today that belied any interest he might pretend in Priscilla."

"Do not be silly, Jane. Priscilla is the daughter of a duke and will have a generous dowry. I am the daughter of a duke's younger son who has little money, and no one has mentioned the subject of a dowry for me for years."

"But do you not want to try to win him back?"

"Do schemes like that ever work? Do they ever bring happiness?"

"Will you ever know until you try?"

"Jane, it is most exasperating to have a question answered by another question!"

"I could not agree more. I am merely copying your techniques of argumentation, my dear Norrie. I will ask you more questions tomorrow after you have thought more about your answers."

Six

For the first part of their journey to Chelsea from Mayfair, Jane watched the passing panorama of London activity with undisguised fascination. "Busy, busy. Everyone is hurrying somewhere. Where do they all find their purposes?"

Eleanor laughed. Seeing the city through fresh eyes was a delight. Everything Jane did, from admiring a silk chemise to dancing her first waltz, brought a new cascade of approbation and gratitude. She could not offer her appreciation often enough.

Today, however, Eleanor was pleased to have an activity for which she could profoundly thank Jane. "I am looking forward to meeting Mrs. Tifton."

"So am I." Jane patted her reticule, in which she had letter of introduction to Mrs. Tifton from one of her favorite teachers from the academy. "In fact I feel a bit of nerves, for I am anxious to make a good impression on her."

Mrs. Tifton wrote articles for a journal devoted to pedagogy, articles that had earned her a good reputation among those devoted to the education of the common folk. Eleanor, too, looked forward to hearing more about her ideas.

The elegant Branden House carriage looked

almost out of place as they reached the outskirts
of the village of Chelsea.

When the coachman pulled the horses to a stop
before a small house, Eleanor saw a young fellow of
fifteen or so waiting for them to arrive.

"Mama," he shouted before he hurried up to admire the horses.

Mrs. Tifton appeared in the doorway without
delay and greeted Eleanor and Jane with all civility.
When they were seated in her modest parlor, Mrs.
Tifton introduced her three children, and the eldest girl brought them tea. They quickly disposed
of the usual courtesies and began their discussion
of modern education, with Jane's congratulations
to Mrs. Tifton on her latest article advocating the
instruction of very young children.

Mrs. Tifton talked about the need for schools in
the very smallest villages, for teaching children to
read before they were required to do work in the
fields or sent off to serve others. "I believe reading
and writing should be rights for every child."

Jane agreed. "Miss Milford and I are trying to put
your ideas into practice."

Eleanor nodded. "But, I am sorry to admit, I am
ill prepared to be a teacher, compared to you two.
I was encouraged to have accomplishments such as
playing the pianoforte and stitching a pretty sam-
pler. Mostly for the purpose of being a good
conversationalist I was taught a bit of history and
geography. Of course any interest I might have had
in Greek or Latin or advanced mathematics was discouraged, even punished."

Mrs. Tifton patted Eleanor's hand. "The state of
education for girls is a disgrace, for girls of all

classes. I predict there will come a day when we females will want to know more about science. I myself have tried a few experiments in chemistry with an associate of my father's, but that had to stop when I married. Did you attend school, Miss Milford, or were you educated at home?"

"I had a governess and shared some lessons with my cousins. Their tutor did not mind spending an hour or two a day with the girls of the family."

"Your parents did what they thought best for you by preparing you to contract a superior marriage."

"Yes, as shortsighted as that appears now."

"Miss Wilson, I know you studied at Miss Carlton's Academy."

Jane smoothed out her skirts. "Before that, my father supervised my education and that of my sisters. He had a few boys from the gentry boarding at our house and prepared them to enter Eton or Harrow."

"You both had the opportunity of living in situations where education was valued. So few children have that advantage." Mrs. Tifton went on to tell them about the schools in which she helped to train teachers to assist in parish schools.

Eleanor was almost brought to tears thinking of the needs of the children, both back at home and here in the city. The children of Branden needed her, and she believed in them. She felt a surge of pride at their accomplishments and a corresponding sense of mission for the work that yet had to be done. Once she disposed of her duty to get Priscilla betrothed, she would not allow any more impediments to deter her. She was eager to return to Branden-under-Wrotham. There was the place her life had real purpose.

* * *

As he entered the dining room, Griff was too intent on scanning the newspaper Bellows handed
him to notice his mother. Until she spoke.

"Griffith, dear."

"Why good morning, Mother. What brings you
downstairs so early?"

"I want you to come to me in the morning room
as soon as you have finished breaking your fast."
Lady Edenhurst, who must have been waiting for
him in order to secure the appointment, patted his
shoulder as she left the table.

"I have an urgent appointment—" Being alone
with his mother was devoutly to be avoided.

"You have an important engagement every day.
I promise our conversation will take a very few
moments."

"As you wish, Mother."

He took a swallow of coffee and let its bitter heat
sear his tongue. Ordinarily he was able to flee the
house before the countess had arisen. He had been
expecting something like this, a tête-à-tête in which
she quizzed him about his intentions regarding
Lady Priscilla. But he had not been quick enough
to escape her today. He had better come up with
some topic to divert her from the discussion of his
marriage prospects.

He pushed his plate of beef away and reached for
a piece of toast. Yesterday afternoon at Branden
House, Bobby had caught him outright, without a
doubt.

Griff had been caught off guard then, too.

Sitting with Norrie had reminded him of that

evening he knew he loved her, a memory always lurking in his mind, especially since she had revealed the reason—or lack of a reason—she had prevented him from approaching her father about making an offer for her hand in marriage.

As Griff remembered it, they had left the dancing behind and gone to the balcony overlooking the shrubbery of someone's summer residence on the outskirts of London. In the distance, a serene lake reflected a silvery lopsided moon, near full. A pair of shadowy figures crossed the lawn, apparently heading for an assignation at the lakeside folly.

He had taken her hand and invited her to stroll in the moonlight. They walked to the river, to the center of the high curved bridge. He recalled the occasional hoot of an owl, the muffled giggling from the folly.

At the crest of the bridge they again had stopped, side by side, not touching, but aware of one another as if a celestial vibration placed them in harmony.

Later, he laced his fingers through hers and brushed his lips across her mouth. At that moment he had been certain she loved him, would welcome his offer. Now he knew he had been too eager, had asked too soon.

With a deep sigh, Griff pushed away from the table and went to his mother.

She looked up from reading a letter. "What are your engagements today, Griffith?"

"Bobby Bates and I are promised to Branden House for an afternoon devoted to charades and riddles."

"Ah! I am glad to hear it, though why you associate with that fellow Bates I cannot comprehend."

"Bates is a loyal and dependable friend, Mother. And I value his company above most others."

"Perhaps you should be moving beyond your friends from the war or your geographic duties." She tapped her finger on the letter. "This missive comes from Harriet's mama. She asks to be remembered to you and wishes to know—"

A knock sounded at the door, to Griff a most appreciated interruption.

Cook stepped into the room holding her sheaf of receipts. "Milady?"

Lady Edenhurst waved her away. "My apologies, Cook, for not notifying you of the postponement of our duties. I shall call you presently."

Cook bobbed a curtsy. "Thank you, Milady."

The countess held the letter to better light from the window. "Now where was I? Mrs. Green asks me to . . . oh, here it is. She asks if you will have her son for shooting this year at Edenhurst. But that request is simply an excuse for her to seek information on your progress toward choosing a bride. Which is, my dear son, precisely what I wish to—"

Griff shook his head. "To say this topic is premature would be a great understatement, Mother."

"But you have been in Town for two months or more."

"Yes."

"Why you should dilly-dally when you seem to be well favored by Lady Priscilla—"

A footman cleared his throat as he stood in the doorway. "Mrs. Smithers."

Harriet went directly to the Countess to bestow a kiss. "Auntie. Griffith. Good morning."

Griff grabbed the opportunity to dodge the rest

of the conversation. "Your servant, Harriet. Mother, we shall converse again soon." Bowing, he strode from the room, grabbed his hat and left the house.

A narrow escape. But he could not resist his mother's wishes much longer, not if he were to honor his promise of allowing her a say in his choice of a bride.

He needed to talk to Norrie again, but finding a moment alone would be a challenge. What was she thinking now? Like everyone else, did she think he would make Priscilla his bride? He needed to know her feelings, if she might be able to grow fond of him again. The signs were few and far between, but he prayed she still had some regard for him.

Had not her escape from their talk at the ball been accompanied by her tears? Had not she said she wanted him to offer for her again? In the drawing room, had not she looked at him in a way that momentarily seemed to be a look of love, of yearning?

It was not much to go on, this wishful thinking, but it was all he had.

Jane sat at the table, her pen poised above a sheet of paper with many lines crossed out. "What is a word that rhymes with *large*?"

Eleanor had not made a mark on the clean sheet in front of her. "*Barge. Charge.*"

"Neither of those will do. Let me see. *Days, haze, lays, ways.*"

"To rhyme with *large*?"

"Do not be a widgeon, Norrie. I am giving up on large and starting over."

"Maze, stays."

"What? *Stays?* We cannot use such words or we will have the company in an uproar."

"Wait until you hear what Hartselle will come up with. He loves to shock."

Jane bent her head and started a new line.

Eleanor fought off a sigh. She had lost her enthusiasm for this afternoon's gathering. Griff was sure to come, for Bobby would not miss an opportunity to sit near Jane and tease her gently.

If only she had not run away when Griff had tried to talk to her they might have . . . might have what? When she did not know her own mind, how could she have told him how she felt?

But the most pressing question she had to address was the one that hurt the most. Could she live with the ache in her heart if Griffith became a suitor of Priscilla, if he developed a serious interest in her silly cousin?

She had made her decision long ago and she was satisfied with it. She loved the school. If she had given up the possibility of loving a man and having children of her own, she might have the appreciation of the boys and girls in the village and the gratitude of their parents.

Above all else, she wanted her children and her school and her life at Branden. She was satisfied with it. Of course she was.

The romantic story with which she passed a few wakeful nights now and then could have been some novel. A hero called Griff, a character of fiction, with only the slightest connection to the man himself. An intricate story of lost love, just a fig-

ment of her imagination elaborated upon until it
had no relation to reality.

Griff, the real man instead of the dream, had
come into her life again. Did that mean anything
beyond adding infinite complications to her mission for the dowager? Did the real Griff Preston,
now Lord Bromley, share anything besides his good
looks with the man she had created in her dreams?
Sadly, circumstances prevented her from getting to
know him, other than as a suitor to her cousin. She
had no choice but to redouble her efforts to drive
all thoughts of him from her mind and avoid him
everywhere.

Jane held up her paper. "Listen to this. Wait, Norrie! You have not written a word. How will we start
the proceedings if we do not have a few puzzles to
begin with?"

"I am thinking."

"Think harder."

"I shall." Eleanor headed the page *Heartache*.
Carefully she wrote, *My first is most essential, the font
that gives one life.* She crossed that out. *Life* too obviously went with *wife*. *That keeps one hale.* She tore the
sheet in half and crumpled the upper part.

"Norrie?"

"I had a foolish idea." She bent her head over the
blank half.

Jane smoothed out the discarded half and gasped
when she saw the word at the top. "Oh, Norrie!"

Eleanor was surprised at the number of people
who gathered in their drawing room that afternoon
to play charades and riddles. She had suggested the

idea to Priscilla as an antidote to the girl's growing boredom. As Eleanor told Jane that morning when they folded the last of their newly written charades, "The Prima, after six or seven weeks on the town, shows disturbing hints she might revert to her old reckless and improper ways at any moment."

Of course, Griff had accompanied Mr. Bates to Branden House. Charades hardly seemed like a pastime either of them would enjoy, but Mr. Bates would probably use any excuse to be near Jane. Eleanor simply had to ignore Griff, pay no attention to him. Accustom herself to his presence without caring.

Now, as the fifteen or so people listened, Eleanor announced the rules. "We will form into four teams. Each team is charged with creating riddles and charades in verse. When you have composed your presentations, we will hold the competition. I will score each team one point for guessing the answer and two points for each team that was stumped. If there is a tie, we will have a final round and watch the time. The fastest team will win."

The guests counted off and assembled into four teams.

Eleanor called for quiet. "I will start the proceedings with a charade Miss Wilson and I made up this morning, just to get the game underway."

She unfolded the first sheet of paper. "Here is the first riddle, good for one point. Who is speaking? Write down your answer."

Of all the maids I was the pearl
My beauty left him in a whirl
To change all England, church and wife

He dared to risk all kinds of strife.
For me, a pretty, witty girl.

As the teams whispered among themselves,
Eleanor watched Griff's head bend toward Priscilla's
pale blond curls. How had they happened to turn
up on the same team? She noticed that Mr. Bates
had managed to be partnered with Jane, even
though Jane refused to participate in the opening
round since she had helped to write the verse. Mr.
Bates seemed to be spending more time gazing at
her than trying to come up with an answer.

After a few moments, Eleanor clapped her
hands. "Everyone done?"

The teams called out their solutions.

The words, "Queen Charlotte," brought a round
of laughter.

One answer, "Marie Antoinette," brought a spate
of oohs and aahs.

"Anne Boleyn," another voice offered.

"Oh, of course! Changing the church!" Mr. Bates
shook his head in mock disappointment.

Eleanor nodded. "Yes, Anne Boleyn is correct."

Everyone spoke at once, commending the com-
position, challenging the witty designation, or
asking just how pretty she was reputed to be.

Eleanor waited for the tumult to quiet. "One
point for each team that was correct. Now you have
a quarter hour to make up your charade and riddles. I know many of you have come with ideas in
mind, so I hope you will not exceed the time limit."

The room was quiet while everyone worked.
Eleanor walked to the window. Though the afternoon was misty, summer was quickly approaching.

She wished she could slow the passage of time, give herself more time. However much she longed to go back to Branden and see her father and the children, she was determined to fulfill her promise to the dowager. The very existence of her school depended upon her success.

She turned to see Hartselle writing quickly, then showing his work to Violet, who giggled and nodded. "I am finished and ready for the fray!" he announced.

Soon the other teams were also prepared, and Eleanor asked each in turn to read a puzzle.

Miss Sanderson stood and read:

"I come from an exotic place
My trumpet always plays the bass
My nose is very long and sways
My ear a giant fan portrays
My tail can wag and wave around
And when I walk I shake the ground.
Who am I?"

When the teams had written their answers, Eleanor called for the solutions.

"I know," cried Priscilla. "A giraffe!"

Lord Peters shook his head. "No, no. The nose is long, not the neck. This is an elephant."

"Correct, very good." Eleanor scored the round, then called on Hartselle, who stood and bowed to the company with an inflated flourish.

He cleared his throat and read in an affected tone:

"Once there was a fellow so fickle
His amours kept him in a pickle,

Whose tastes were so very exotic and bold
He covered himself in silver and gold.
His name you will find on a roster quite royal
But some of his subjects were never too loyal.
Who is he?"

The question brought gasps, giggles, and not a
few outright guffaws. Some looked aghast, others
grinned.

Eleanor rolled her eyes. "I suspect you are very
naughty, Cousin Hartselle."

"Not in the slightest!" With a superior grin, he
seated himself again beside the duchess.

Eleanor waited only a moment. "Dare we ask you
to read your answers aloud?"

Priscilla was anything but reticent. "What is
wrong with saying the name of the Prince Regent?"

Everyone laughed, then silence fell as all eyes
turned to Hartselle.

Making the most of the moment, he paused and
looked from one to another. "Any more guesses?"

No one spoke.

"Well, I proclaim I am astounded to have flum-
moxed everyone. You are all two centuries off. The
fellow I wrote of was none other than Charles I!"

Applause rippled around the room and Hartselle
made another of his very deep bows. "Never let it
be said that a Stuart is less than a German when it
comes to extravagance!"

These were, Eleanor thought, the moments that
made Hartselle a welcome guest everywhere in
town. He was often audacious, almost disrespectful,
always outrageous.

Eleanor waved the company to quiet once more.

"Only Hartselle and Violet's team wins points for that round. I do not know who will dare to go next. Any volunteers?"

She was amazed to see Mr. Bates stand and nod to the assembly.

"I composed this charade last evening, so Miss Wilson may be excused if it does not meet your approval. Here it is:"

> My first is nothing but the best
> A flower favored o'er the rest.
> Second is the very start
> Of beauty growing from the heart.
> My whole is graceful, prized, and so
> Look quickly now. I soon shall go.
> What am I?

The murmur of whispering filled the room.

Eleanor ran over the words in her head. Whatever the answer, the poem was beautifully romantic. Did Mr. Bates intend it more for Jane's ears than the rest of them? Jane's cheeks were certainly quite pink, and she gazed at Mr. Bates as though he were a messenger from heaven.

"Tell us the answer," Hartselle demanded. "Your eloquence has put us all in the shade."

Mr. Bates walked to a table and took a stem from one of the flower arrangements. When he turned around, he wore a wide grin.

"The answer is this." He handed Jane a delicate pink rosebud. "Rosebud."

"Thank you, Mr. Bates." Jane's words came in a breathy whisper as the others applauded all over again.

Eleanor hated to break the spell, but eventually she had to call on another reader.

The remainder of the afternoon's activities passed in a blur. Eleanor was anxious to speak with Jane, to learn just what her friend thought of Mr. Bates's extravagant gesture. She could hardly wait for everyone to leave.

Once they finished arguing about the final scores, the party moved into the dining room for a cold collation.

Eleanor should have felt triumphant at the success of the afternoon. Jane and Mr. Bates were inseparable, even over their plates of food. Eleanor ought to be satisfied with her capacity to take no notice of Griff. Or, to be honest, to notice him less than she usually did. This was progress, indeed.

As Eleanor said farewell to most of the guests, she realized that Mr. Bates and Griff were still sitting with Jane. Priscilla excused herself to go upstairs and rest before changing for their evening's engagements.

Jane called to Eleanor. "Norrie, may we go into the library and show that old atlas to the gentlemen? Mr. Bates is exceedingly anxious to see it."

"As am I," Griff said.

Eleanor flinched. She had completely forgotten about the wretched old atlas.

Griff watched Norrie enter the library, her demeanor completed changed from her smiles in the drawing room. At the moment she looked miserable as she perched on the edge of a chair, keeping her eyes lowered.

Miss Wilson directed a little frown at her, but

Griff could tell Norrie did not notice. What had changed in the few moments she spent saying good-bye to her guests? He feared she was uncomfortable being in such close quarters with him, and if so, he wondered at the implication of her distress.

Somehow Lady Priscilla had arranged to be his partner in the game, and a worse collaborator he could not have imagined. He doubted they had earned half the number of points the others had. But how was Eleanor to know he had not schemed to put himself at Lady Priscilla's side?

All the more reason for him to speak to her in private.

Jane urged Eleanor to show them the atlas. "Norrie found this here in the library."

Norrie pushed the book forward on the desk, staring at it intently. "I believe it must have belonged to my great-great-grandfather."

"May I?" Griff asked, reaching for it.

She grabbed her hand back as if he held a red-hot poker. "Why, yes, what good is a book if it is not read and admired?"

That bit of spirit sounded to Griff more like the Norrie he knew. He opened the book and read the title on the elaborate title page. "Take a look at this engraving, Bobby. A masterful example of the printer's art of those days."

Jane stood and peered over Bobby's shoulder. "Look at Neptune riding a sea monster off Cornwall."

Bobby slowly turned a few pages. "Each county is illustrated with coats of arms and a compass rose."

"Who are the figures on some of the maps?" Jane asked.

"I am not certain, but some of them appear to wear ecclesiastical robes."

Griff glanced back and forth from Norrie to Bobby and Jane. He could tell Norrie had difficulty restraining her natural enthusiasm and keeping quiet. "Have you seen Speed's work before, Bobby?"

"We have some of his maps at the institute, but none this old. Ours come from an edition done in 1676."

At last Norrie spoke. "What do you know about him?

Bobby answered as he examined each page with care. "He was attached to the court of Elizabeth I, and apparently traveled around the country for many years."

Jane moved a chair close to Bobby's and concentrated on the book of maps. Bobby was equally absorbed.

Griff turned to Norrie and spoke softly. "Can you guess the value of this atlas?"

She looked up, surprise evident on her face. "Value? You mean if we were to sell it? I should never do that!"

"Would the duke?"

She gave a little gasp. "I cannot imagine such a thing. And there are probably many volumes here even older and perhaps worth far more. This is the library of the Dukes of Branden. Like the estate, I should think it could never be sold."

"There was an auction just last week of pictures and books from some house in Essex. I believe the Prince Regent bid on a number of paintings."

"That makes me very sad."

He leaned toward her, let his urgency sound in

his voice. "Norrie, I am trying in my very awkward
way to make the point that conditions change.
What seemed unthinkable one day might make
good sense on another."

"I do not understand."

"Let me begin again. If there is any hope for me
to win your regard again, I want to—"

"Shush!" Norrie's cheeks flooded with color as
Jane's head bobbed up for a moment then quickly
bent to the book again.

"Step outside with me for a moment, please."

Norrie pressed her hand to her lips. "I cannot."

"You must!" He rose and drew her after him into
the dim corridor outside the library, closing the
door behind them with a quiet click.

Her face had returned to that granite stiffness he
hated to see. "Lord Bromley, I believe that all of
London Society sees you as a suitor of my cousin,
Lady Priscilla. That is how I regard you as well."

"But, Norrie, can you not see that Priscilla and I
would never suit, while you and I can recapture the
love we—"

"Stop! I am a teacher and I take my duties seriously. I have obligations to my father, my school,
to Branden-under-Wrotham, to all the Branden
estates."

"What can I do to convince you?"

Her eyes were hard and cold in the faint light.
"You cannot change my decision. But if you want to
help me in some way, stop coming here to see
Priscilla."

"But I never come to call on your cousin, Norrie.
I come to see you."

"Oh, no!"

Was her voice a cry or a moan? Before he could grab her, she whirled and ran to the staircase, pausing only a moment to look back at him before she fled up the steps. Griff knew he detected the gleam of a tear in her eye.

Deuce take it, no school ought to come between Norrie and him! That argument was too flimsy to stand.

Seven

In the morning, Eleanor knew the truth. She should have run right back down the staircase and thrown herself in Griff's embrace. Her whole body yearned to feel his strong arms wrapped around her. What a fool she was to run away again, just as he said the most romantic thing she had heard in ages: He came to call on her. On her, not Priscilla.

For hours after she had crawled into her bed last night, she rehashed the encounter with Griff, trying alternative endings of various emotions, various sensations, anything but the one she had enacted. Sleep finally took her back to the same old dreams, fantasies of what might have been.

In the bright light of day, she feared she had sealed her fate with Griff. And her cousin's, too.

"I do not expect to see Lord Bromley calling upon the Prima again." Eleanor and Jane were alone at the breakfast table.

"Whatever happened between you? He came back into the library looking as haggard as an old crone and simply sat there until Mr. Bates and I gave up on studying the atlas."

"Oh, Jane. I hope Mr. Bates will come to see you even if Lord Bromley stays away."

"He might come back to look at John Speed's atlas again. He wanted to study it more."

"It is quite clear that you and Mr. Bates have developed *tendres* for one another."

Jane wrinkled her nose. "We have been acquainted only a few weeks."

"And how much longer do you need to know him to ascertain his suitability for you? He has a profession and, according to Lord Bromley, a reasonable income. What would your father and mother say to losing you?"

"I have hardly given it a thought."

"I do not believe you." Eleanor looked Jane straight in the eyes.

"Why not? Just because a male and a female spend time together does not mean they are destined to wed."

"It is by far the best evidence."

"Pooh." Jane sipped her coffee.

"So you are immune to Mr. Bates's charm and good nature?"

"Well, perhaps not entirely immune. But there is a great leap between enjoying his company and imagining oneself as his wife."

"But I am willing to wager you have been indulging in just such imaginary thoughts from time to time."

"Oh, Norrie, I wonder if I could be a wife? I have been so long a dutiful daughter and a proper teacher, I wonder if I could serve a gentleman and live under his protection?"

"If you love him . . . if you care for him, why not?"

"I could ask you exactly the same thing, could I not?"

Eleanor pushed away from the table. "You could ask, but I could not answer."

Eleanor went in search of an apron, scissors, and a waste receptacle. The flowers in the drawing room were in urgent need of sorting, trimming, rearranging, and, in some cases, disposal. To begin with, she untangled all the wilted blooms and stripped the sagging leaves and blossoms, halfway filling her bucket with discards. She stood back to survey the depleted vases.

As she began to trim a curving white spray, Pratt announced a caller. "Lord Blythe, Miss Milford."

She turned around and dipped a little curtsy to his bow.

Lord Blythe had an engaging smile. "Please excuse my inappropriately early call, Miss Milford. I am sorry to interrupt your activities, but I beg a few moments of your time this morning before the rest of the household is present."

Eleanor put down her scissors, removed her apron, and took a chair. "Please sit down, my lord. How may I help you?" She remembered seeing him at various routs, perhaps at Almack's. He had called at Branden House before, but not often.

Lord Blythe wore the near-uniform of the Corinthian set, precise as to the cut of his coat of blue superfine, the handsome folds of his white cravat, the mirror shine of his tasseled Hessians.

He seated himself and adjusted a cuff. "Miss Milford, I have been much absent from social occasions for the past weeks. Regrettably I was frequently away from the city, rather preoccupied with matters at my estate in Kent." He paused to let a dazzling smile play across his face.

This was a man well aware of his appeal to the ladies, Eleanor thought. *He has set about charming me!* "I trust that you were able to satisfactorily see to your responsibilities, Lord Blythe."

"Indeed, to the satisfaction of all, I presume. However, I fear I am not *au courant* with the status of this Season's *amours.* I solicit your advice, Miss Milford, on the affairs of your lovely cousin, Lady Priscilla. Are her affections as yet engaged by one of her many distinguished suitors?"

The more Eleanor looked at Blythe, the more she wondered about him. She wished she could come right out and ask his age. He might be a bit too old for Priscilla. Or perhaps those little lines about his eyes resulted from a life outdoors. On the other hand, the fashionable pallor of his skin made that unlikely.

Lord Blythe went on. "I would not wish to hamper an alliance that is well on its way to fruition. If Lady Priscilla has found her ideal mate, I shall not attempt to press my suit. If, however, she has not yet chosen among her admirers . . ." He let his words hang in the air.

"Of course I cannot speak for Lady Priscilla," Eleanor said.

"Naturally not. But you are well placed as her chaperon to know better than any other what her feelings are."

His voice, smooth and oily, did not please Eleanor's ears. On the contrary, she found him far too practiced, too glib. His meticulous courtesy seemed excessive, as though a cover for a slightly rakish background.

But she was not choosing a suitor for her own

tastes. Lord Blythe's air of sophistication might be exactly what Priscilla would want. The hint of a faintly racy background was a contrast to Griff's refinement.

"My lord, I cannot guarantee she has no secret partiality. I suggest you see for yourself if she welcomes your attentions. Is that a reasonable answer to your request for information?"

"Reasonable indeed. I greatly appreciate your time, Miss Milford. I hope to be seeing you often in the days ahead."

He stood and made a bow almost as exaggerated as Hartselle's, then took his leave.

Eleanor could not put her finger on the exact quality in him she mistrusted. Too shrewd by half, perhaps.

She put the apron back on, picked up the scissors, and again contemplated the row of vases with their depleted bouquets.

Nothing seemed to fit with anything else. She scooped up the flowers, tossed them all in the bucket, and rang for the maids to remove the empty vases.

Griff tossed the newspaper on his desk. He stalked to the window and looked out, only to see his mother stepping down from the carriage. In just a moment she would be here regaling him with the chatter of the afternoon's calls.

He loved his dear mother, but today his head ached with his convoluted thoughts about Eleanor, Jane and Bobby, Priscilla, and the fact he had not found any more young ladies that suited his fancy though he had attended a score of balls, not to mention scads of other social activities, assemblies, even the dreaded nights at Almack's. The fact was, he wanted no one but Eleanor and the only reason he spent an instant in Priscilla's company was to be near the woman he had loved for six years. Now she had shut him out of her house.

No wonder his head felt like a vise was tightening against his temples.

"Griffith?"

"Yes, Mother?"

Lady Edenhurst bustled into his library. It was nearly as old as the Duke of Branden's. He wondered if somewhere among the shelves of books there might be another copy of the Speed atlas. He had never examined most of the books here. They belonged to his father, and then were to go to his brother. For all practical purposes, now they were his.

Lady Edenhurst removed her gloves and handed them to Bellows. "Griffith, I have had the most wonderful idea."

He waited for her to go on.

She looked at him quizzically. "Do you not want to know my idea?"

"Of course, Mother. I am eager to hear it." Nothing could have been further from the truth.

"I am going to invite Lady Priscilla and the duchess to Edenhurst for a week. I think later this month will be perfect. All the roses should be in bloom and . . ."

"You will what?" He could not believe his ears.

"Violet agrees with me, and even though she is far from strong, she will come along—with Miss Milford, of course. And Jane Wilson, if she is still in town."

"Mother!" Griff was entirely speechless.

"If Priscilla is to become your consort and the eventual countess, she should certainly see the estate. The repairs you effected last fall make the house almost perfect again. Violet wants to see it, too."

"You mean you have already issued the invitations without discussing it with me?"

"The visit may give you an opportunity to be alone with the dear young girl. I have been watching, and I have not seen you even escort her outside alone for a breath of air. You are often with her, but always in company."

"I thought you ladies were too eagle-eyed to allow a young lady to be alone with a man."

"Of course we are. But there comes a time in a courtship when a few moments of privacy might be expected. With all propriety, that is!"

Griff's head pounded and the vise seemed to have tightened perceptibly. "I do not think this trip is well advised, Mother."

"I feared you might disapprove, darling. That is why I am arranging it all myself. I knew you would not presume to think Lady Priscilla would want to come to Edenhurst when the Season is winding down. But the duchess declares Lady Priscilla most assuredly wants to see your estate."

"There is no possibility of rescinding the invitation or postponing the visit?"

"Now why would you want to do that? Just leave everything to me."

As she marched out of his library, Griff dropped his head into his hands. Things were far worse than he had expected.

* * *

"You accepted an invitation for Priscilla to spend a week at Edenhurst?" Eleanor sputtered in indignation.

Violet lifted the lid of her tiny vinaigrette and waved it under her nose. "We will all go, even Miss Wilson. Lady Edenhurst says it will be a lovely little respite for all of us."

"Does Priscilla want to leave London now? The Season is almost over, and she will miss some of the premier events. As her chaperon, I would recommend postponement."

"Ah, Eleanor, I know you have done everything for dear Priscilla, but as her father's wife, I must assert myself."

"Violet, if she goes to Lord Bromley's estate for a week, other gentlemen will assume the obvious. Has she decided to make a match with Lord Bromley? That was not my impression."

"Eleanor, please, think of my nerves. I declare I shall soon be having spasms again. I am much too delicate for this disagreement. Please humor me just this once."

Eleanor wanted to shake the stuffing out of her uncle's wife. But how could she raise a ruckus when Violet always claimed dissension made her ill?

She must find a way to prevent the visit. It would be a disaster. Even for the Prima, it made no sense.

But when she broached the subject, expecting Priscilla to be as anxious as she was to prevent the trip, Eleanor received a jolting surprise.

"I think a few days away from the *ton* might be just the thing. There are several gentlemen who take me quite for granted. If I seem to favor Lord

Bromley, some of them might come up to scratch, as Mr. Bates termed it."

"As I have told you many times, Priscilla, cant phrases sound very amusing out of the mouths of gentlemen, but spoken by a lady, cant expressions are simply crass, in bad taste, and improper."

"Well, that is what the men say, you know."

"Which does not make it less improper."

"I suppose you are correct. You know, Eleanor, I expected I would have several prospects from which to choose by now. Not one single man has asked me to marry him yet. Or asked to approach Papa, which is how you said the process begins. I am very discouraged. Though that very handsome Lord Blythe paid me special attention last evening."

"So he did."

"Even though I do not wish to make a match with Lord Bromley, he is a pleasant gentleman. I think a week away from London might do me some definite good."

"I disagree, Priscilla. A few carefully placed hints would do quite as well."

"Nothing we do matters anyway. Violet has already accepted Lady Edenhurst, and no matter how many complaints Violet makes about her frail constitution, when she makes up her mind to do something, she cannot be deterred."

Eleanor knew Priscilla was correct.

"Can you get away from town for a week, Bobby?"

"Why would I want to do that?"

"To help out an old friend in need of the support of his comrade."

"That is you, I take it?" Bobby blew a cloud of smoke and twirled his cigar between his fingers.

"Who else?"

"You ain't my only friend, Bromley. Maybe the best, but not the only."

"I need you, more than I can say. Mother and the Duchess of Branden have concocted a little visit next week to Edenhurst for themselves, Lady Priscilla, and Miss Milford."

"What!"

The strength of Bobby's exclamation caused assorted frowns and disapproving mutters from some inhabitants of the otherwise hushed coffee room.

"I know, I know." Griff kept his voice low. "Before I even knew what was happening, those females arranged the whole thing, behind my back."

"Put a stop to it immediately. Refuse to go. Whose house is it anyway?"

"Edenhurst belongs to father, though he will certainly have nothing to say about the party. What good would it do for me to refuse participation? I cannot be so discourteous as to humiliate my own mother."

"I have a connection with the master of the horse. How about a summons from royalty to prevent your compliance?"

"Robert, I have to go. Much as I regret the necessity, I see no alternative."

"And my role would be as court jester?"

"Yes. No. You will keep me from being the only male present, other than my father, who never leaves his bedchamber anymore."

"Griff, I will be honest. Your mother is an exceptional lady. Miss Milford is a fine person. But that duchess does nothing but whine whenever I have the misfortune to be in her company. As for Lady Priscilla, I believe a few more years in the barrel would improve her mellowness and depth."

"Not a bad analogy, Bobby."

"Anyway, while they all are away, I can call at Branden House and study that atlas. Perhaps in the company of the charming Miss Wilson."

"Who will be at Edenhurst. Did I not tell you that?"

"Most certainly you did not. In that case, I shall accompany you with pleasure."

"May I say that ravishing the daughter of a vicar on my premises is beyond the limit?"

Bobby answered with another guffaw, followed by a second round of mutters.

Griff stood. "Let's find a less solemn spot to seal our bargain."

As they left the club, Griff saw Lord Blythe heading for the card room.

Bobby saw him, too. "You never told me about that Blythe fellow."

"He is a scoundrel who deserves the censure of polite Society."

"He does not look out of the common way."

"Appearances often lie. I knew him in Portugal before you arrived. I saw his real character, or lack of it. He was known as Clarence Green then, a lieutenant. He was in charge of the supply lines at the rear of the battle. Instead of tending to his duties, once the troops moved forward, he occupied himself with assaulting the women in the camp. He was shot attempting to seduce his commander's wife, of all things."

"Where did he come by the title?"

"Some distant uncle, but no money came with the barony. According to my sources, he is eager to make a match with a wealthy heiress and forge a connection with a highborn family. He is an obsequious toadeater of the first order."

"Why do people receive him? I thought Society was so fussy about acceptable persons."

"He flaunts his war wound, never revealing the injury was result of a guard shooting him when his victim screamed. If the man had not been such a rotten shot, he would have died spread-eagled on the poor woman. As it is, he merely has to sit down carefully."

Bobby chuckled.

"Blythe is fortunate only a few of us knew of his disgrace. He has hidden his nature from all Society, I believe. He spoke to me about never revealing my knowledge the first time I walked into White's, begged me to keep quiet. He said he was confident I would avoid spreading knowledge of his youthful indiscretions."

"Indiscretions? I think seducing the wife of your commanding officer might merit a stronger appellation than indiscretion."

"The man is a fool, in my opinion, and liable to fall prey to some fortune-hunting woman who believes his boasts and traps him."

"But you will not reveal his secret?"

"Not unless he makes it necessary."

Eleanor fastened a tiny silken flower into her hair. "The fun of a masquerade is that you can be someone else for a little while. Which is precisely why you must help me keep track of the Prima this evening."

They were almost ready to depart for one of the highlights of the London season, Lord and Lady Wyntend's annual Shakespearean Fête, for which everyone dressed as a character from one of the Bard's plays.

Eleanor pinned another flower over her ear. "Ordinarily I would refuse to allow Priscilla, in her first Season, to attend a costume ball, but this one is very special. All the music, the dances, the games, the refreshments follow the Elizabethan theme."

Jane ran her fingers over the midnight black of the flowing silk domino airing on one door of the tall armoire in Eleanor's bedchamber. "Will she try to escape us?"

Eleanor shook out the sleeves of an identical domino on the other door. "I do not know. We will carry these with us and if Priscilla tries to steal away from me, we can put them on and hide ourselves in the crowd to keep track of her."

"How sneaky you are, Miss Milford." Jane wagged a finger at Eleanor.

"I suspect she tried to give me the slip several times, but I kept her in sight and made sure she knew it. There are several fellows who might try to maneuver her into a compromising situation. Priscilla thinks a forbidden kiss sounds very romantic and good fun. But she risks ruining her reputation or, at the very least, becoming the object of gossip. Grandmother would show her no mercy. Nor would I."

Jane peered into the cheval glass and rearranged the wisps of hair on her forehead. "I thought that trick of coaxing someone into compromising situations only happened when females tried to trap unsuspecting men, not the other way around."

"For a young lady reputed to be an heiress, like the Prima, the same game can be played."

"Oh, I see. But, Eleanor, I thought you said the duke had not decided on a specific dowry.

"Few know that. Most probably assume the amount will be generous, given the duke's holdings."

Jane fluffed up her hair in the back. "I truly feel like a fairy! Am I supposed to be Pease-blossom or Cobweb? I forget what we said."

"It matters not to me. Pick one."

Jane pondered a moment, then nodded decisively. "I shall be Pease-blossom. I have always coveted a name more colorful than plain Jane."

"Then I am Cobweb."

"Remind me of Priscilla's costume."

"Cleopatra. From the tragedy *Antony and Cleopatra.* I warned her that Cleopatra dies at the end of the play, but the story makes no difference to her. She finds Cleo a romantic figure. Actually she wanted to be a mermaid at first. I told her there were no mermaids in Shakespeare, but she would have done it anyway if she could have figured out how to do the tail and still be able to dance."

Jane shook her head. "Sometimes the Prima is thicker than a castle wall. Before Lord Bromley left for Sussex, he told Priscilla that if he were to come to the ball, he would wear an ass's head and call himself Bottom. She did not catch his meaning, but I fell into a fit of the giggles. Has Mr. Bates gone with him?"

"I understood he would ride down tomorrow. He wanted to stop along the way to visit a cousin. Just for an hour, he declared, for her children are active and numerous."

That evening, by the time their carriage negotiated the congestion near the Wyntend residence, Eleanor and Jane had pointed out several possible Romeos, a tall Othello, and a female they assumed was the murderous Lady Macbeth.

"Part of the fun," Eleanor explained to her cousin, "is to identify the characters."

Priscilla grimaced. "But you know how I hate to read Shakespeare."

Eleanor bit back her response and let the remark go unanswered. She dared not look at Jane for fear they would break into laughter.

Fortunately they were quickly caught up in the stream of people entering the house, a Mistress Quickly on Falstaff's arm, a Hamlet carrying a skull, and a lady whose costume of a simple nightgown could have made her Juliet or Ophelia. The house was filled with people, as befitted one of the Season's most anticipated events. In the crush they could not reach the staircase to ascend from the ground floor, but nevertheless were soon separated.

Eleanor found a bit of breathing space in the dining room, where she encountered Lord Blythe, who bowed as low to her as the crush of the crowd would allow. They exchanged comments on their costumes, his being a velvet doublet and short cape.

Lord Blythe replaced his hat. "I am Orsino, Duke of Illyria, but if your fair cousin comes as Juliet, I shall call myself Romeo instead."

Eleanor tapped his arm with her fan. "Then, my

fine duke, you shall keep your name tonight. I will not give away Lady Priscilla's costume or character, but you will know her without hesitation."

She saw the feathered hat on tall Lord Peters pass the doorway and excused herself to overtake him. He wore a deep green velvet cloak that hung to his knees.

"Good evening, Lord Peters. Have you seen Lady Priscilla?"

"Yes, she was just here, but I believe she went off with Miss Sanderson, who needed some repairs made to her costume."

"Ah. Thank you. In this press of people, I have lost her. You are looking very distinguished in your costume." She spoke the truth, Eleanor realized. The fine raiment gave Peters a solid look, perhaps a hint of how he would develop as he filled out in maturity. The gangliness that characterized his physique seemed no longer evident.

Lord Peters hooked his thumbs under the edges of his fur-trimmed lapels. "I thought I should be a traveler, one who goes off to interesting places and expands his horizons. Valentine travels from Verona to Milan."

"Is that your ambition?"

"Yes. I long to see all of Italy. To glide along the Grand Canal beneath the Rialto bridge. Or stand near the Duomo before Ghiberti's magnificent doors. There are so many treasures in the world, Miss Milford. When the war is over, I long to see them for myself. I should like to go as far as Egypt."

"Have you talked with Priscilla about your ambitions?" Eleanor wondered where Priscilla got the idea to be Cleopatra.

"I have told her of my dreams. And I have reason to believe she understands, one of the few people who agrees with me."

Apparently his father still opposed the travel. Jane waved at Eleanor through the crowd of people. "Excuse me, Lord Peters. Miss Wilson seems to need me."

"I shall see you again soon, Miss Milford."

Eleanor wove and ducked her way through the throng to meet Jane.

"Priscilla was drinking champagne in the ballroom with a handsome fellow all in black, perhaps a quarter hour ago."

Together they fought their way up stairs and slowly wove their way to the ballroom.

The set was just ending and Eleanor saw Lord Blythe again, this time at Priscilla's side, standing very close and taking full advantage of the opportunity for a close look at the flimsy bodice of her costume.

Eleanor put a hand out to stop Jane from moving any closer. "I think we should wait and watch."

A masked figure in a red domino suddenly appeared next to them, bowed, reached for Jane's hand, and wordlessly led her out to the newly formed set.

Eleanor forged on alone, chatting with acquaintances and staying within sight of Priscilla. When her cousin danced, Eleanor relaxed and found a cup of lemonade. When Priscilla moved to the other end of the room, Eleanor threaded her way from one cluster of brightly garbed figures to another to keep track of her. The strain of the effort made Eleanor long for an end to the proceedings, no matter how amusing it was to listen to the lute or watch the unusual figures danced. Even Eleanor's best slippers failed to prevent her feet from aching as the evening drew to a close.

Jane found Eleanor just after the last tune was played. "I am breathless. I had no idea those Tudors worked so hard at their dances."

"Tell me who you danced with."

"Oh, Eleanor, Mr. Bates was clever indeed. We danced two sets with him all covered up in the red robe. Then he removed it and we danced again. I think he was supposed to be Henry the Fourth. I thought we had to stop dancing to keep attention away from ourselves, but then I remembered I had the other domino in my reticule so we finished the evening with him wearing black. Not that anyone would have paid the slightest attention to me!"

Eleanor laughed out loud. "Oh, Jane, my dear, your bow to propriety is very comical. Here I thought you had captured the hearts of many gentlemen."

Lord Blythe escorted Priscilla to Eleanor and Jane. "If the day is fair tomorrow, may I take you ladies for a turn around the park?"

Priscilla shook her head so vigorously she almost dislodged the dark wig. "How very sorry I am to tell you we are leaving town for a week to visit in Sussex. After we return, I will gladly ride in the park with you."

"That would afford me great pleasure, Lady Priscilla. I wish you a pleasant journey."

When they were settled in the carriage and moving toward Branden House, Jane related a funny scene between an Othello and a fellow claiming to be Iago. But Eleanor paid little attention.

Letting Priscilla see more of Lord Blythe was mildly distasteful for some unknown reason, probably nothing more than her excessive caution. But before she dealt with that problem, there was a week of constant proximity to Griff to contend with. The Season was finishing up without any evidence of an ideal candidate for Priscilla. The thought of going home to admit defeat to Grandmother gave Eleanor a chill deep inside.

Eight

The Branden traveling coach drawn by the duke's fine team made short work of the distance from London to deepest Sussex. As soon as she glimpsed the gentle green hills of Edenhurst, Eleanor recognized the place from her dreams. She felt as familiar with the old beeches, the massive oaks, the emerald lawns as if she had been here many times. For six years, she had taken what Griff said about his home and embellished the images into a paradise more lovely than the countryside around Branden. Now she knew the pictures in her mind were accurate.

Above the canopy of trees, a few wispy clouds danced across the bright blue sky. An ancient stone wall bordered the road, occasionally decorated by cascades of shiny green ivy. From time to time in the distance, she could see sheep grazing and lambs playing. Idyllic indeed.

Eleanor needed to keep her admiration under the same strict control she kept her sensibilities for the remainder of this week. Violet and Lady Edenhurst would do everything possible to ensure a match between Priscilla and Griff, though neither of the potential marriage partners was amenable. If they could make it through this week without falling prey to the marriage scheme, Eleanor would be relieved. As for her own feelings for Griff, she needed to make that rigorous control permanent! This awkward visit could not be over soon enough.

In early afternoon, they passed through the tall gates and soon spotted the mansion from the long winding driveway. The gentle breeze rippled the ribbons of her bonnet as she leaned her head out of the window to see the house. Eleanor remembered that Griff had said the house was almost two centuries old, but it looked much newer, in the neoclassical style popular for the last few decades.

Griff, Lady Edenhurst, and Mr. Bates waited for them on the front step. After making apologies for the earl, who was too ill to see guests anymore, they soon had the duchess and Lady Priscilla escorted to their accommodations.

Eleanor and Jane, to share a room, awaited the return of the housekeeper.

"I cannot believe this house is so old," Eleanor said. "It looks as modern as any I have seen."

Griff nodded. "They say the plans were probably drawn by Inigo Jones while he was surveyor to Charles I. He was as pure a Palladian as Lord Burlington and his followers, though Jones's ideas were later overshadowed by Wren and a host of baroque and Jacobean builders."

Bobby gestured to the stately columns in the entrance hall. "Burlington rediscovered the principles that Jones practiced."

Once they were settled in their bedchamber, Eleanor stared out the window and watched Griff and Mr. Bates mount horses and ride away. They had explained they were staying at Bromley Manor, a much smaller house a few miles distant on the land of the original barony.

Jane stepped up beside her in time to see the two horsemen disappear around a bend. "Do you know anything about architects, Norrie?"

"I fear that is another of the gaps in my education. I feel certain we can begin to remedy that lack while staying at this house."

"Sometimes I am faced with the fact I am a poor excuse for a teacher. The more I learn, the more I realize I do not know."

"I feel the same, Jane. The men mentioned three names I know we should recognize. When I have a moment I am going to inform myself about Jones and Burlington. I know Wren built St. Paul's Cathedral, but beyond that, I am in the dark."

Eleanor hoped if she kept her mind on learning new subjects, the time would pass quickly.

Priscilla's pretty face wore a look of complete boredom as she stood in Lady Edenhurst's still-room the next morning. Priscilla heaved a sigh and let her head loll to one side.

Eleanor smiled silently to herself. Exactly as she had predicted to Violet, Priscilla wished she was back in London in the middle of the social whirl, not listening to the countess's recital of necessary skills for mixing useful household concoctions. Eleanor noticed Lady Edenhurst did not mention the illness of her husband, for whom her potions must not have been effective.

Lady Edenhurst gestured with her spoon. "This

mortar and pestle I reserve for the herbs from my own garden."

Violet had not accompanied them to the still-room. Hardly a surprise, Eleanor thought. Violet never went near the stillroom at Branden. Lady Edenhurst had promised to bring the duchess a mixture of feverfew, comfrey, and thyme, which she guaranteed would ease Violet's megrims.

The countess Edenhurst did not appear to notice Priscilla's indifference to her instruction. "Tomorrow morning we can arise early to gather the roses before the dew is dry. I like to hang them upside down for a week to ten days before stripping the petals. Later on tomorrow, we can make some rosewater with dried petals Dora collected last week. Then we can see if the rosemary has progressed enough, but I imagine I shall have to do that job later in the summer. You see, Lady Priscilla, timing is everything when working with herbs and flowers."

Eleanor knew her cousin had a total lack of appreciation for the older woman's knowledge.

In one of her cupboards, the countess had several rows of bottles labeled with their contents. She removed several, explaining each step to the inattentive Priscilla. Lady Edenhurst opened her stillroom book and paged through it to the receipt she sought, then measured several of the liquids into a jar.

Jane watched intently, the stillroom being one of her favorite places. "May I copy your receipt, my lady?"

"I should be most pleased if you would, my dear."

Priscilla rolled her eyes and drummed her fingers on the counter until she caught Eleanor's frown and tried to put a smile back in place.

Lady Edenhurst did not detect Priscilla's grimace. She stirred the potion and poured it into a small bottle. When it was tightly stoppered, she wiped her hands and announced herself satisfied. "I think her grace will feel much better if she takes a few drops of this mixture every few hours."

Norrie drew Priscilla aside as they left the still-room. "You and I need to have a talk."

An hour later, they excused themselves and went upstairs to Priscilla's room.

Priscilla sat at the dressing table and gazed at herself in the looking glass. "I know what you are going to say, Eleanor, and you will be correct. I insisted on making this visit and I deserve to be bored to flinders."

"Precisely. But you need not make your aversion to household duties so obvious to Lady Edenhurst."

"If I married her son, she would learn soon enough how little I care for such things. But since I probably will not accept an offer from Lord Bromley, it should hardly matter."

Eleanor felt a lurch of her heart. Priscilla had never before come so close to removing Griff from her list of suitors. "Lady Edenhurst is well known in London circles, Priscilla. If she takes a dislike to you, she might well make her views known to other ladies, perhaps the mothers, sisters, or aunts of other gentlemen you hope to impress."

"Are you always so logical, Eleanor?"

Eleanor shook her head. "Not always." In fact, she felt like jumping for joy at that very moment, not the most logical reaction to Priscilla's suggestion she might eliminate Griff as a prospect.

* * *

Griff sat at his father's bedside, watching the old man sleep.

He stretched his legs out and leaned back into the chair, trying to comprehend how his affairs had become so complicated.

His father stirred, opened his eyes, and raised himself on one elbow.

"Father?"

"James. Where have you been?"

"I am Griffith, not James, Father."

"Ah." The old man lay back on his pillows.

He often mistook Griff for his elder son, whose death came as a new blow every time the earl awoke.

Slowly Griff led him through the familiar questions and answers, the moans of recollection as Lord Edenhurst again endured the pain of hearing of his loss as if for the first time. A greater burden Griff could not imagine.

After more than half an hour, the earl was reasonably lucid. "Help me to sit by the window."

Griff assisted his father the few steps to a chair well positioned to view part of the garden.

"You say you have guests? Who are they?"

"The Duchess of Branden, Father, the duke's second wife. Lady Priscilla, his youngest daughter. Miss Milford, the duke's niece, and her companion Miss Wilson."

"Why are they here?"

"Mother and the duchess are scheming to make a match between Lady Priscilla and me, but I fear the young lady is looking for more of a man-about-town, a Corinthian."

"She pretty?"

"Yes. But too often pouts."

"Hear me well, son. Listen to your head. And your heart. Even loveless marriages can last a very long time." He heaved a great sigh.

Griff dared not pursue the implications of that statement. While the earl was lucid, he needed information. "Father, many years ago I recall you mentioned that there are drawings of this house. They might have been done by Inigo Jones."

The old earl raised one hand in a helpless gesture. "James never cared about Bromley or Edenhurst and their history. I always thought someday he would be interested." A tear slipped down his cheek.

Griff knew he should leave the old man alone now, but he pressed on, eager for the information. "Do you know where the drawings are?"

"I wanted him to love Edenhurst."

"James did love the estate, Father. And I love Edenhurst, too. I have pledged myself to the care of the land and the tenants, all the crops and the cattle. Try to remember, Father, where those drawings are kept. If you please."

"In the estate office." The old man wiped his eyes with the back of his hand, and Griff gave him a clean square of linen.

The earl sighed deeply. "No, wait. Not the office. In the library."

"Where in the library? I have looked through the cabinets and drawers."

The old man was drifting off to sleep. "The library . . . in the library."

Griff vowed to find them. Too bad he could not start immediately.

* * *

The afternoon of their first day was devoted to a walk around the grounds of the estate. Eleanor felt quite energetic, ready for a brisk walk as they gathered in front of the south façade. She felt sure that by the end of this visit, Griff would drop any ideas he had about marrying the Prima.

Griff nodded toward the house. "The ground floor is of rusticated stone in the Italian manner, as they built in the Renaissance."

Eleanor quickly looked at Priscilla, whose frown was evident to all of them. She moved closer to the girl and gave her a concealed poke.

Griff dropped the subject anyway. "Forgive me, ladies, for beginning with a rather dull topic. I sometimes get carried away with my interest in this house. There is a bit of a mystery about it."

"Mystery?" Suddenly Priscilla's attention was engaged. "Never say there are ghosts."

Griff shook his head. "Nothing at all Gothic. No clanking chains, chilling moans, or specters in the attics. The mystery is the identity of the original architect."

Priscilla's voice revealed her disillusionment. "Oh, how disappointing."

They walked some distance on the lawn and looked back at the house. Eleanor found it pleasing, its harmonizing stones of gray and pale tan showing a hint of sparkle in the sunlight. A well-balanced balustrade of lighter stone capped the façade. "Is there a roof walk?"

Mr. Bates held up a hand as if to stop the question. "Take care, Miss Milford. Lord Bromley has a way of enticing people up there to view the garden scheme from above, and I can testify to the steepness of the stairs."

Jane gave a little sigh. "I am sure the vista is worth the effort."

Griff clapped Mr. Bates on the shoulder. "You see, Bobby, you have just enlarged the tour's itinerary. You shall have to suffer those stairs yourself or abandon your duty to these fair ladies."

They walked farther and again stopped to observe the house against the background of the wooded hills. The proportions of the building gave it nobility, not its size, Eleanor thought. "The name of the architect was Inigo Jones?"

Griff shrugged his shoulders. "So it is said. He did not design many houses, but he had a career of prodigious accomplishment. Supposedly he drew sketches for this house, but they have been lost. I have hosted visits from several experts who have come to argue over the features of the building, but who find no conclusive evidence one way or the other."

"How unfortunate you cannot find the drawings." Eleanor watched Griff as he looked back at Priscilla. His expression gave no hint of his feelings.

"Father says they are somewhere in the library, but I have searched and cannot find them."

"There are five of us. Perhaps we could look again."

Griff rubbed his chin. "Not a very exciting activity for you."

Eleanor began to feel eager for the search. "On the contrary. If we help, every nook and cranny can be examined again."

Griff's forehead wrinkled in a frown. "If everyone is willing . . ."

"Did you look among the leaves of every book?"

"Not every one, I suppose."

When they returned to the house, Griff took them to the library. "We might try this for a while, if all of you are agreeable."

Mr. Bates looked around the paneled room. "You could coax me with a glass of sherry, Griff."

"I shall join you later," Priscilla said. "I will sit for a time with the duchess."

Griff was all politeness. "I am sure she will welcome your companionship, Lady Priscilla."

Eleanor watched his expression carefully but saw no clue to his thoughts about being instantly abandoned by the girl.

Jane scurried off to find cloths to use as aprons to protect her dress and Eleanor's.

Until dinner, helped by a round of sherry, they worked their way through dozens of books, ruffling the pages of each but finding nothing.

Griff thanked them all for their assistance. "Perhaps we can continue tomorrow for an hour or two."

"Oh, yes," Eleanor exclaimed. "I find this activity quite enjoyable."

Bobby laughed. "You see, Griff? Never let it be said you don't know how to entertain a lady!"

The next morning after breakfast, the sun having been wiped away by a heavy cloud cover and the threat of rain, Eleanor suggested they resume their search of the library. Lady Priscilla joined them.

Her half smile looked sincere. "You are looking through all of the books?"

Griff waved to shelf after shelf. "Perhaps the sketches were tucked into one of these books as a hiding place and were forgotten. If we find the drawings, we might solve the question of who designed the house."

"Oh. I see."

When all the arrangements were at last in place and Priscilla had a supply of books at hand, silence fell over the group. Griff concentrated on the shelf nearest the desk, probably the most convenient place for someone who sat here frequently.

Half hour later, Priscilla, who had been desultorily leafing through several volumes of engravings, spending more time looking at the pictures than seeking their quarry, stood up and announced she thought she would take a rest from the books. "I see it is not raining. I think I shall take a little turn about the garden, Lord Bromley. Do you wish to accompany me, Eleanor?"

"I do not think that necessary. I shall stay here and keep looking."

"Just stay away from that overgrown maze," Griff warned. "Even from the roof of the house we might not be able to find you if you get lost inside. It has not been trimmed for many a year and it is full of thorns."

"I shall stay far, far away." Priscilla removed her makeshift apron and left the library with a look of relief on her face.

For a few moments the silence was broken only by the sound of pages turning or papers shuffled in cabinets.

Bobby slammed shut a large volume. "Griff, how did your maze get full of thorns?"

"Actually, there are very few thorns. But it is over-grown, a tangle of wild branches, and I am afraid Lady Priscilla could really become lost . . ."

Bobby grinned. "But she will not go there be-cause she would not risk getting her dress torn? You are a devious fellow, Lord Bromley!"

"In the case of Lady Priscilla, I believe that would be a clever fellow," Eleanor said, almost under her breath.

Griff smiled. "Thank you, Norrie, ah, Miss Mil-ford."

Again the silence was punctuated only by the rustling of paper. An hour passed, then another.

After interrupting their work for luncheon, they returned to the library, leaving Priscilla to read the new issue of *La Belle Assemblée* with the duchess and Lady Edenhurst.

Not even a third of the books had been examined, though most of the cabinets had been thoroughly searched. Griff had again questioned his father, but received no more useful hints as to the whereabouts of the drawings.

By mid afternoon, Griff decided their work was no longer efficient. "All of us need a brisk walk after we have a cup of tea. I fear we are wasting our time."

Eleanor disagreed, but truly felt eager to be out of doors. "We can try again in the morning, when we all are refreshed. May we see more of the gar-dens this afternoon?"

Griff nodded. "Indeed, though I fear you may be disappointed. Large areas of the original plan, the outer gardens, have been allowed to grow wild, as has the maze and the area around the grotto."

In the drawing room over the refreshments, Lady

Edenhurst agreed. "I fear we have been more concerned with the earl's health than the shearing of the hedges and the cultivation of the parterres. A pity, but without constant nurturing, gardens get out of hand."

Behind the words, Eleanor thought, was a great deal of melancholy.

Lady Edenhurst summoned a smile. "Lady Priscilla would undoubtedly find many hours of great pleasure in contriving the restoration of the gardens."

Priscilla pretended not to hear, from all appearances.

Eleanor and Jane exchanged amused glances. If the Prima knew the difference between a daisy and a tulip, it was only because of the bouquets for which she had to write her thanks in London this Season.

Nor would Violet have given a rap for the gardens herself, Eleanor mused. If it were not for the dowager, the Branden gardens would have long ago been taken over by weeds.

As they headed for the water gardens, Lady Priscilla lagged behind.

"Come along, Priscilla," Eleanor cautioned.

Priscilla indulged in a whine, though she kept her voice low enough not to be heard by the gentlemen. "I went for a walk this morning, all alone because the rest of you were looking at those old books. Is there not a village we can visit?"

"You may ask Lord Bromley, but if you do not walk a little faster, they will leave us far behind.

Nearing the first in a series of ponds, Priscilla grabbed at Eleanor's arm and gave a little shriek of pain, sinking to the grass.

"What is wrong, Priscilla?" Eleanor instantly suspected a trick.

Griff, Mr. Bates, and Jane turned back.

"Lady Priscilla! What happened?" Griff came to her side, but Priscilla waved him away.

"I have twisted my ankle. I must have stepped in a hole!" She began to sob.

Eleanor and Jane exchanged a knowing look. The accident was too expedient to be genuine.

Griff took Priscilla's hand. "Can I help you arise?"

Eleanor wanted to shove him out of the way and demand Priscilla stop her make-believe. But she did nothing to keep him from crouching down beside the tearful girl.

As Eleanor could have foreseen, the efforts of both Griff and Mr. Bates were required to make Priscilla comfortable, to offer her a series of options for returning to the house and to assuage her tears and pain. Eventually, Griff lifted her into his arms and carried her all the way back to the house, Mr. Bates at his side.

Lagging far behind with Jane, Eleanor snorted in disgust. "What a revolting exhibition of fake agony! She did that entirely on purpose."

Jane watched Griff attain the edge of the lawn. "Perhaps we should have followed along and tripped him. Then she might have had an actual injury."

"Another bravura performance by the Prima. But we should not be surprised. I knew she would not find this visit to her liking. Lord Bromley is a man of considerable accomplishments and knowledge, not at all the kind of man she truly desires as a husband."

Abruptly Jane started for the house, grabbing

Eleanor's hand and towing her along. "Hurry, Norrie. We must get the Prima straight to bed and wrap that ankle so tightly she will not be able to stand on it for days."

Eleanor scurried along in Jane's wake. "Maybe Lady Edenhurst has some wonderful potion that will make her sleep for the rest of the week."

"I have a receipt of my own!" Jane exclaimed.

"Be careful, though. We do not want to extend this visit beyond our invitation. She must be willing to walk soon."

When they met in the Crimson Room before dinner, Griff inquired about Lady Priscilla. "How is our invalid?"

Norrie did not smile. "I do not expect her to wake for dinner."

Jane did not hide her amusement. "Your mother and I gave her a tonic to help her sleep. Violet took some, too."

Norrie let a tiny grin play about her lips. "I predict that Priscilla will be cured by morning and Violet will beg for more."

Griff joined Bobby in a chuckle, cut short when his mother came in.

"The duchess was overcome with sympathy for Lady Priscilla. She will not be able to join us tonight."

Eleanor could see Jane shared her opinion that not an honest word was spoken as they all offered their regrets at missing both ladies.

Conversation at the table flowed freely as all five present indulged themselves in questions and observations about the house.

Eleanor was full of questions. "I believe you called the Crimson Drawing Room a cube, Lady Edenhurst."

"Yes, for the width of the walls and the height of the ceiling are in perfect accord."

Griff formed the shape of a cube with his hands. "If you double this, as though two cubes stood side by side, you would have the dimensions of the State Drawing Room, a double cube. There are several rooms such as these that Inigo Jones is reputed to have designed. The proportions are precise and typically classical in the style of the ancient Romans, and as repeated in the Italian Renaissance."

"It is said to resemble Wilton House, though I myself have never ventured all the way to Wiltshire to see for myself," Lady Edenhurst said.

Eleanor was fascinated by the mathematical aspects of the designs. "I have read that some proportions, typically the ratios of height and width used by the classical builders, are actually more pleasing to the eye than unsymmetrical designs. Was that the theory behind Jones's work?"

Jane had read the same essay. "Human beings feel more comfortable in spaces with agreeable dimensions, or so one expert speculates."

All agreed the theory made sense. When the butler brought the bottle of port to Lord Bromley, the three ladies excused themselves.

Lady Edenhurst led the way. "Let us go into the Double Cube Room and test the theory of comfort for ourselves."

Griff poured Bobby a glass and filled one for himself. "We do not need to linger here, for I suspect you wish to hear more of Miss Wilson's observations."

"I do indeed. But I have a question to ask you. And let me preface it by saying that all I heard from you about your home did not prepare me for this house and its grounds. Seeing it and the extent of the estate gives me a new appreciation for your concerns. Not that I doubt you can make a success of it."

"The most ironic part of the situation is that I find Bromley Manor exactly to my taste. As Miss Milford was remarking about proportions of buildings that make their inhabitants comfortable, I could not help thinking that Bromley is a perfect size, an old house with the church and barns dating from the fifteenth or sixteenth centuries. Nothing grand or haughty about it, just good English traditions built into every beam. For all of the magnificence of Edenhurst, I find only the library has the feeling of a room in which you can slip out of your boots, slump into a chair, and take an afternoon nap."

"You have a good point there, Griff." Bobby gestured to the painted ceiling above the long polished dining table. "All of this is fine now and then, but for me, even a house like Bromley Manor is too imposing."

Griff sipped his wine. "I actually spent most of my childhood at Bromley. The house has been kept in use by the earls' first sons. We lived there while our father was the baron. After he became earl, my brother left the manor uninhabited. He preferred living in Town. I thought you had a question."

"I do, but stop me if I am raising a subject you wish to forget."

"Go on."

Bobby set down his glass and looked Griff in the eye. "What happened to your brother? How could he have thrown all this away after he was raised to have it all?"

"James was always a careless fellow, took risks he should have ignored. He and his friends gambled and wenched and tried to see how much trouble they could create. He was constantly the cause of great concern to Mother and Father, but they were always proud of him and they believed that someday he would grow into his duties and fulfill all their goals for him."

"But he thought only of himself?"

"I am sure he would have changed as he aged. We were very different, as I suspect all heirs and their younger brothers are. I made my own way with much less attention and a great deal more liberty. Everyone watched out for what James would do. No one cared what I did, and I was glad. I believe James envied me."

"Given your comparative positions, I believe I would have, too."

"He died in that most foolish of all ways, as part of a nonsensical wager on a curricle race. The wheels tangled and he was thrown out at a fast rate of speed and broke his neck."

Bobby shook his head slowly. "Then the story I heard was accurate."

Griff looked thoughtful. "Yes, as I am learning almost every day, even the most devastating events can happen by chance." Griff pushed back his chair and stood. "I think we should join the ladies before I grow more morose."

Eleanor felt tiny under the high coved ceiling of the Double Cube Room. Far above her, buxom goddesses, their gowns covering only a small part of their charms, and spear-wielding gods in armor prepared for battle. They were accompanied by chubby pink cherubs against a background of blue sky and billowing clouds. Elaborately carved panels alternated with blue silk hangings and vast tapestries on all four walls. The furniture, grouped around the fireplaces, stood on thickly woven carpets of many colors.

Lady Edenhurst must have noticed her guests' fascination with the room's decor. "To the best of my knowledge, this room has been preserved exactly as it was when the house was new. We replaced the rugs a few years ago, and I am sure the silk has been refreshed, but otherwise, all is original."

"I find it magnificent," Eleanor said. "Simply magnificent."

Jane made a sweeping gesture. "I agree. I would call it baroque in feel, almost more like what I have been reading of Wren than Jones."

"Griff knows more about them than I do." The countess moved a little closer to the fireplace. "This is a room for entertaining large numbers of people, which we have not done for many years."

When Griff and Bobby joined them, Eleanor and Jane peppered them with more questions until the clock chimed eleven and they noticed the countess had drifted into a little nap.

At breakfast, Priscilla was able to hobble to the table with the help of Eleanor and a footman. Eleanor watched her bask in the attention of all, just as though they believed she truly suffered. Only Griff's mother's expressions of sympathy had the ring of honesty, she thought with a chuckle.

Griff helped Priscilla to a chair. "I am gratified you were not seriously hurt."

"I am sure I shall be fine in just a day or two."

Eleanor suggested another round of searching for the drawings of the house, and all agreed. Even Priscilla seemed glad of the company in the library as they methodically leafed through each book on the shelves.

After an hour, Priscilla wished to go back upstairs. "My ankle has begun to throb."

Jane patted her knee. "Would you like more of that draft I gave you yesterday? If you are asleep you will not be bothered by the pain."

"Oh, please, Miss Wilson. I would appreciate your help."

"Do you need me, Priscilla?" Eleanor asked.

Jane answered for her. "I will help her, Norrie. You stay here."

Griff assisted Priscilla out of the room and Jane followed, stopping for a moment to wink at Eleanor.

Bobby carried a pile of books back to the shelves and replaced them in their original positions. "Miss Milford, you may stop me if my prying is too inquisitive, but I am curious about your feelings for Griff. He is my best friend and I think you are all that is best for him."

Eleanor tried to shrug off the question. "I am the chaperon, and Priscilla is the lady to whom Lord Bromley pays his addresses."

"Humbug, Miss Milford. You may try to pretend that is so, but we both know the situation is otherwise."

"Then perhaps, Mr. Bates, you should explain things to me. As you see them, of course."

"Gladly. A long time ago, before he went to war, Griff fell in love . . ."

"How did you know?"

"He told me so himself."

Eleanor was stunned, but said nothing.

"Now when I met the young lady he once loved, I saw exactly why he could not forget her. But both of them are proud and stubborn and rather silly, whatever pretensions they have for erudite discussion about architecture and such."

"If you think this sounds familiar to me, I assure you I know you are making up this story and shaping the details to fit some matchmaking idea you have."

"Think what you wish. I was saying these two people are mulish and harebrained."

Eleanor could not stop herself from giggling.

"He is letting other people order him around because he is not sure what she wants. She has convinced herself that her own feelings are secondary to the whims of her relatives. Now contrast my friend Griff and his lady friend with another couple I know."

"Who are they?"

"Oh, never you mind their names. This man has long been a bachelor who never wished to alter that state. He met a lady who was new to London. They like each other and have no reason to deny it. Both of them are happy and content. Which story makes the most sense to you, Miss Milford?"

Eleanor laughed, but she saw his point. "Since I do not know who the second couple could possibly be, Mr. Bates, I cannot offer an educated view. I feel sorry for Lord Bromley and his friend, however, for

I suspect there are many complications missing in your version of the tale."

"Perhaps. But their overriding concern should be for their own happiness."

When Griff and Jane returned, Eleanor continued to look through volume after volume. But she thought carefully of the last remark about caring for their happiness. It was simple, yet important. And in everything she did, she needed to keep it in mind.

After another hour of fruitless searching, Griff sounded discouraged. "We are almost half done with all the books. But I am beginning to think this is not the right approach. The drawings must have been considered valuable. Perhaps they were hidden with more forethought."

"Are there any secret panels in here?" Jane asked.

Bobby jumped to his feet. "I suppose that is the answer, Miss Wilson." He and Griff felt around the edges of the shelving and tapped on the paneling to seek a hollow spot. They continued around the room until they had covered every inch of paneling.

Eleanor watched them from time to time, but continued to leaf through each book on the second level of shelves. "The earl was certain they were in this room?"

Griff sadly shook his head. "That is what he maintained, but I am not sure his mind is clear enough to recall their exact whereabouts."

"Is there another likely place?"

"What about in that clock?" Jane asked.

"Or perhaps in the globe. It must be hollow," Eleanor offered.

Bobby opened the clock doors while Griff examined the large globe in the corner of the room.

Griff's face broke into a wide grin. "I say, it does seem to have hinges, right along the equator!"

Bobby quickly went to his aid, and together they lifted the globe out of its pedestal and set it in a chair. They found the tiny latch and opened it. Eleanor and Jane crowded round to peer inside. At the bottom of the cavity, there sat a packet of papers carefully wrapped in linen.

Griff lifted them out and put them on the desk. "Whatever these are, someone took care preserving them."

As he unfolded the cloth, he gave a little gasp of triumph. "Here they are, the drawings of the house. And other buildings."

One by one they looked at the drawings, seven in all, a single sketch of the south façade, another of the north side, a detail of a pilaster, two drawings of decorations Griff recognized from the double cube room, and two outlines no one recognized.

Griff smiled triumphantly. "This is certainly the view of this house, the south façade. But none of them are signed." Eleanor felt a stab of disappointment. How sad to find them only to be once again without definite proof.

Griff looked carefully at the paper with the fewest sweeps of the pen. "I believe this is the edge of the design on the wall panels in the cube room. We shall have to compare it later."

Mr. Bates peered at each drawing. "I am certain if we examined the decorative panels inside the house and out, we would find these designs were used over and over again in several places. The pilaster looks familiar to me."

Jane looked crushed. "Now, though you have the drawings, the mystery remains."

Griff shook his head. "The mystery is greatly reduced. There are experts in London who can compare the type of paper used, the style of the drawing, the curve of the lines, even the ink, with others known to be the work of Jones." He took a magnifying glass from the drawer of the desk and looked more closely at one of the sheets.

He put down the glass. "Or the experts might conclude the drawings were made by several men, some associates or students of Jones. He must have been a busy man, and probably had a host of helpers."

"What other buildings did he design?" Jane asked.

Griff gazed at one of the drawings, his face reflecting his satisfaction. Even his voice was full of enthusiasm. "The Banqueting House in Whitehall, the Covent Garden square, many others, most of which remain today. He also designed the costumes and scenery for masques held at court, a very popular pastime for the Stuarts. The Banqueting House was the place the masques were held."

Eleanor expressed her surprise. "You mean he designed for the stage where the purpose is to create the illusion of reality, and he also built these grand stone buildings, too?"

"Yes, as contradictory as that seems, he did."

Eleanor studied one of the sketches. It seemed nothing more than a few lines on a scrap of paper, almost the portrayal of a tangle of yarn from the upside down view. But when she turned it around, the outlines of a scrolled entablature was clear.

Jane asked the crucial question. "Are you disappointed, Lord Bromley?"

"No, indeed. I am pleased we found the drawings, and I have every confidence they will add to the knowledge about Jones. We may never make an absolute attribution of this house to Jones, but no one can doubt his influence upon the design. The drawings add to the knowledge. And best of all, Father will be pleased and delighted."

Nine

As usual when Griff settled on the chair beside the bed, the earl was still asleep.

The events of the previous days had been nothing like Griff had expected this house party to be. Instead of strolling with Priscilla and fighting complete boredom, he had discovered the lost drawings and had some delightfully promising discussions with Norrie.

Priscilla's behavior was that of a young and impulsive girl, and he could not rebuke her for that. He and Eleanor had been just as foolish a few years ago. Priscilla exhibited the same flair for melodrama that had sent him off to war without a good-bye. What a nodcock he had been!

After her theatrical fall, carrying the young lady had not been much different than hefting his field equipment up hill and down. For his part, Griff had no way of knowing whether Priscilla was dissembling or not. He rather guessed she had not meant to cause quite the commotion that followed her accident, though she very likely had fallen on purpose. Eleanor and Jane certainly thought so.

The earl sighed and began to awaken. It had become almost a routine, always painful, but less so every day for Griff to see his father slowly experience each step of his return to full awareness. Whatever kind of brain fever afflicted him, the awful truth had to be learned again every time he awoke.

It might have been better, Griff mused, if he had no ability to comprehend reality at all. He could be spared the daily rediscovery of his eldest son's death. He could be spared the comprehension of his own weaknesses, his inability to manage his life, his state as a prisoner in a failing body. Only for a few hours each day did he have control of his thought process. It was a tragic way to end a useful life.

For his father, it was especially sad and lonely and painful. The earl had tried hard to involve James in the operations of the estate, but what he turned over to his eldest son was often left undone. The land, the tenants, and the whole region surrounding Eden-hurst had suffered for the last few years.

Griff's education had been far different from James's. As second son, he always knew he had to make his own way in the world and so had chosen a profession with care, one he would always relish.

Gradually now, the earl began the slow climb to full consciousness. When the process had completed its sad passage and his father was seated in his chair at the window, Griff told him about the discovery of the drawings.

"In the globe, yes. Now I remember," the old man said. He held the drawings to the light and nodded as he examined each one. "They are exactly as I remember. I was just a boy when I last saw these." He handed them back to Griff. "Take good care of them, James."

"I shall, Father. I certainly shall."

The earl's attention was captured by something he saw outside on the lawn.

"Are those the young ladies your mother is parading for your choice?"

Griff peered over his shoulder and smiled. "Not exactly parading, but yes, they are the ladies who are our guests, other than the duchess, who is probably indisposed."

"Who's that with them?"

"Robert Bates, my old friend. The lady on his arm is Miss Wilson, and I suspect they are falling in love. Lady Priscilla is the golden-haired girl who has a slight limp. She turned her ankle day before yesterday. The chestnut-haired lady carrying the book is Priscilla's chaperon, Miss Milford."

"The second one looks much the better prospect for a comfortable wife."

"I will admit I have entertained that notion as well. She is five- or six- and-twenty, and she is smart, where Priscilla is giddy and silly."

The earl looked at the ladies again and nodded. "As I say, my son, the smart one is a better choice. Those golden-haired gels spend too much time before the mirror."

Or seeking widespread attention to their fraudulent suffering, Griff added silently.

In their room to change for luncheon, Eleanor eased her foot out of her half boot. "Priscilla's limp seemed to come and go, or was that my imagination?"

Jane brushed her hair and coiled it. "I do not think you will have to worry about the severity of her injury causing us to extend our visit. The Prima is more than ready to go back to Town."

"The quiet of the country must seem less appealing than ever to her after the excitements of the Season."

"We can hope that when she returns to London,

Lord Blythe or some other dashing Corinthian will beg for her hand, and all will be settled." Jane anchored her hairpins carefully.

"Yes, she has as much as told me she has decided against marrying Lord Bromley, no matter what."

Jane clapped her hands in joy. "She has? You did not tell me immediately! That is wonderful news."

"She has already changed her mind about several of her callers a dozen times. Her decision could be reversed any minute."

"True. But it might give you cause for hope—"

"Stop! One thing at a time, please."

Jane's smile had the tinge of slyness. "But your imagination must be busy."

"No more than yours, Jane. Are you thinking of your future with Mr. Bates?"

"If—just allow the possibility—if I married Mr. Bates, I would miss the school terribly."

"Yes, I have missed the children for these months away. Those bright little smiles every morning."

"Oh, you will make me weep."

Eleanor shook her head. "If you wish to have a classroom full of children to tutor, Jane, there is no shortage of subjects."

"What are you saying?"

"Wherever there are children, there is a place for your skills."

Jane looked a bit surprised. "I never thought about it that way, but you are quite correct, Eleanor. If one is willing to teach without monetary compensation, as we do, I am sure any classroom would be crowded with eager learners."

"And if one were married to husband with an adequate income . . ."

"Yes, I am sure I could marry Mr. Bates and not give up teaching altogether. The same could be said for you, if you became Lady Bromley."

"Jane! Do not utter such a thought out loud. You know that Violet and Lady Edenhurst are still convinced that Lord Bromley will wed Priscilla."

"But from what I see, neither Lord Bromley nor Priscilla agree."

"Come now, enough of this speculative nonsense. We will be late to the dining room." As they descended the grand staircase, Eleanor could not help allowing just a tiny bit of her imagination to see her as chatelaine of Edenhurst. Someday.

On the final day of their visit to Edenhurst, the clear sunshine beckoned the entire party, with the exception of the duchess, out of doors. The roses had burst into full bloom, drawing the walkers to their admiration. But after a short turn about the rose garden, Priscilla excused herself to return inside, blaming the continued weakness of her ankle. Lady Edenhurst accompanied her back to the house.

Griff laughed to himself. Had his mother not suggested that being alone with a young lady might be the outcome of this visit? Except that the young lady she meant was not the one with whom he yearned to keep company. And it seemed the moment was nearly at hand. If Bobby had an ounce of understanding, he would soon be far away and Jane with him.

Griff and Eleanor strolled quietly for almost a quarter hour before Bobby and Jane wandered away from the roses toward the kitchen garden.

Eventually Griff broke the silence. "I don't think Priscilla has enjoyed visiting Edenhurst very much."

"She wanted to come."

"My mother and the duchess thought they had a match, that is, that I would . . . rather, that she wanted . . ." Now that he was getting to the crucial issues, why was he at a loss for words?

"I know. From that very first afternoon at the Belfour Musicale, people have been trying to marry you to Priscilla."

He chuckled. "Very true."

"Did you ever seriously consider having Priscilla for your wife?"

"No, though there were times when I was quite angry with you for refusing to talk with me. Fortunately, Norrie, I am learning patience."

"Patience is always extolled as a virtue, is it not?"

"Often in short supply in this world."

Eleanor grinned. "Indeed."

They strolled on, out of the rose garden and across the lawn.

"So has the time arrived when we can talk about ourselves?"

She stopped and faced him. "Probably not."

He felt the sting of her words. Her frown gave away both her hesitation and worry. "I shall accede to your wishes, Norrie. But I do not understand why."

They began to walk again.

Eleanor drew a deep breath. "I am very tempted, Griff. Very tempted indeed to ignore my promises and let Priscilla make her own way in the world. Or let Violet take a more active role in finding her a husband. But I cannot do such a thing, at least not yet. Is that enough explanation?"

Griff almost shouted No! but restrained himself. "It is only you I want to be with, my dear Norrie. And where those feelings are concerned, no explanations to the contrary make sense to me."

"Do you mean it, Griff?"

"I do." He took her hand. "Come with me where we cannot be seen from the house."

They hastened to the high hedge bordering the garden, and he led her through the hidden entrance.

Griff pushed back a few branches. "The maze is overgrown, but no one can see into it anymore and we can be alone at its center. There is a bench where we can sit and talk."

Eleanor's heart raced as they hurried along, Griff pushing back the branches that overgrew the path. He turned several times and she followed him blindly, knowing she could never find her way out.

The sunlight filtering through the intertwined boughs gave a green glow to their course. She felt she was in an enchanted place, removed from the real world. Her heart told her she wanted to hear more of his endearments, yet they had so many issues to sort out between them. She had to hurry to keep up with his long strides, and it seemed he turned a hundred corners.

At last they turned into a grassy space and she stopped suddenly. There on the bench, Jane leaned into the arms of Mr. Bates, their lips pressed together in a long kiss.

Eleanor clasped her hand over her mouth to prevent a gasp of surprise. But Griff did not suppress his cry.

"Bobby!"

Jane and Bobby broke apart instantly and looked at their interrupters in surprise, then with sheepish grins.

"What are you doing here?" Griff asked.

"The same thing you apparently came here to do!" Bobby stood and drew Jane to his side. "Miss Wilson has just consented to be my wife—pending the approval of her father, naturally."

"My father will either approve or I shall disown *him!*" Jane sputtered with laughter.

Eleanor broke into laughter herself and threw her arms around Jane. "I am so happy for you."

Jane whispered, "I hope the news bodes well for the progress of your romance."

Eleanor shushed her. "It is not quite so simple," she whispered back.

"Love is never simple," Jane said to all of them. "But love must prevail."

Bobby put his arm around Jane's shoulder. "Now that we have made good use of this special place, my dear, I suggest we leave it to our friends for whatever purpose they have in mind."

"I agree." Jane put her arm around his waist. Pressed together, they started out of the little clearing.

"If we get lost, Griff, do not hurry after us." Bobby threw Griff a last grin as they disappeared into the shrubbery.

For several moments Eleanor did not move, then she walked to the stone bench and seated herself. Facing her and almost hidden in the green branches was the statue of what appeared to be a cherub on a lichen-covered pedestal.

Griff walked over to it and tucked a few branches behind it, letting the cherub's gaze shine unimpeded on the inhabitants of the bench.

Eleanor looked at the winsome smile that played on the statue's lips. He was a charming rascal, that fellow.

At last Griff sat down beside her. "I admit I am surprised. Oh, not that Bobby and Jane are together. Their mutual attraction has been evident from the first time they met. I am surprised he has proposed already. He has avoided the parson's mousetrap for years!"

"She will return home just a few days after we go back to London."

"Yes, the Season is almost over."

Eleanor gave a rueful little laugh. "That is precisely my problem. I need to find Priscilla a match in the next few weeks."

"You *need* to? Why?"

"I have promised my grandmother. She does not approve of my school, you know."

Griff looked confused. "Oh?"

"We made a bargain. If I want to continue my little classroom, I must find Priscilla a husband. She must be betrothed by August, or the dowager duchess will not allow us to teach the children anymore."

"But is this not Priscilla's first Season? She is only eighteen. What is the hurry?"

"Perhaps it is only a whim of the dowager's. But I must say Priscilla is chafing at home. She and Violet would never speak ill of each other, but in truth they do not relish each other's company."

"I am beginning to get the picture more clearly, Norrie. You were dispatched to chaperon Lady Priscilla's entry into Society and find a match for her in order to get her out of her stepmother's hair."

"Bluntly put, but accurate."

"And you thought I might be a candidate for the sacrifice?"

Eleanor made a mock cringe. "Sacrifice? I thought

you might be attracted to her. Priscilla is quite lovely, and she will have a sizable dowry."

"Bah! She might be pretty to look at, but she is hardly mature enough to be the kind of wife I desire."

"Oh."

"The wife I desire is a little older, but equally beautiful. She would have experience teaching school, I believe, and would be devoted to her scholarly father."

Eleanor felt a blush spread across her face. "Griff, would you be able to forgive such a woman for being callow and thoughtless in her youth? For thinking foolishly and making a big mistake, a mistake for which she has never forgiven herself?"

Griff took her hands in his. "Perhaps I was the one who made the mistake, running away instead of trying harder and making my suit irresistible."

Eleanor shook her head. "I fear we are getting into very dangerous territory. Your mother and Violet both believe you will ask for Priscilla's hand and that she will accept. Before we proceed with any conversation about ourselves, we must consider what to do about Priscilla."

"Yes, I see your point. But you know that no one can force me to offer for a girl I do not choose myself. Nor will the opinion of the duchess or my mother coerce me into a marriage I do not desire."

"But you cannot deny the situation is awkward, Griffith. Once we return to London . . ."

"Priscilla does not want to marry me any more than I want to wed her. She is excessively bored here at Edenhurst. My mother and her grace are quite in error if they think she would be happy here. On the other hand . . ."

"Stop! Say no more, Griff. We must be careful and

take things one step at a time. As anxious as I am to talk about us, I feel this is premature. Priscilla wants to be settled this year, too. Time is getting very short, I fear."

"We have already lost six years, Norrie."

"Griffith Preston, you tempt me beyond anything. I would love to toss all my responsibilities to the wind. But what are a few short months to wait after all this time?"

"My dear, I am being thoroughly selfish. There should be no hurry about finding Priscilla a husband. She is very young. Waiting will only do her good."

His deep laughter made her heart sing. He stood and again brushed back the branches from the cupid's face. "Here now, fellow, I ask you to judge who is the better lover today, Bobby or me?"

He sat back down beside Eleanor and took her into his arms. She melted against his chest and surrendered her lips to his.

"My darling, Norrie," he whispered. "I have waited so long for this moment."

"Dearest Griff." She brushed a lock of hair off his forehead, gazing into his clear gray eyes. "You are the man in my dreams." Her voice was barely audible.

"Your dreams and mine must be indistinguishable from one another."

"Yes?" She turned up her face for another gentle kiss.

"Do you realize I could obtain a special license and we could be wed without waiting any longer?"

She pulled away from him. "If we are not to torture ourselves with these thoughts, we must work out a plan to get Priscilla wed. Then we will know we are working toward our own happiness."

"I bow to your superior knowledge of tactics, Miss

Milford." He drew a finger along her cheek and smiled into her eyes.

She shivered in delight. "Stop that. We must be serious."

"I have never been more serious in my life." But he straightened up and clasped his hands behind him.

Eleanor folded hers in her lap. That lock of hair was dangling again. She looked at the grinning cherub instead. "When we return to London, I suggest you continue to call on Priscilla as though you intend to make her an offer."

"But I certainly do not—"

"Part of the reason Priscilla consented to this week at Edenhurst was the urge to create envy in her other suitors, envy that might drive them to hasten their pursuit of her."

Griff took a deep breath and sighed. "Yes, I see her reasoning, but will it work?"

"What can it hurt? If you are still one of her suitors. Perhaps you can also persuade others of her appeal."

"Feign eagerness to win her favor?"

"It might help a little."

"I am in awe of your intrigues, Norrie."

She slipped her hands around his neck and pulled his mouth to hers again.

Ten

Eleanor had to convince Priscilla to accompany Lord Bromley, Mr. Bates, Miss Wilson, and herself on the river excursion a few days after they returned to London from Edenhurst. She used the same argument that had convinced Griff to continue to call upon Lady Priscilla. "Inspiring envy in the breasts of other men is still a worthy objective."

"I thought someone would have been waiting on our doorstep, Eleanor. Charlotte tells me I have a collection of suitors beyond anyone's this Season. But none of them wants to come up to scratch. I mean, excuse me for using the term you deplore, no one has asked if I will be his bride. I am soon to be deep in the sullens."

Eleanor tried to summon some encouraging words. "You are the Toast of the Season, Priscilla. Perhaps some of your suitors are overwhelmed and intimidated by the esteem in which you are held by so many."

Priscilla tossed her head. "Perhaps. But I do not understand why they do not make their intentions clear."

"I am sure of it, if you make your preferences known . . ."

"Lord Bromley did not even try to kiss me."

"Certainly not!"

"Violet said he would once I got to his estate. But I would not accept his proposal anyway. He is too old, too staid, too boring. His idea of fun is looking at an old house, for heaven's sake."

Eleanor, deep inside, gave thanks for the shallowness of her cousin. "Tomorrow evening is the rout that Sir Gavin's sister holds every year. I know you have a new gown to wear. You shall charm all your admirers, I am sure of it. In the meantime, spending an afternoon boating on Father Thames should be diverting."

"I know they will prose on and on about all those buildings. More your sort of thing than mine, Eleanor. But I will go anyway."

Once they disembarked from the boat at Greenwich, Priscilla's mild interest in the river traffic disappeared. She viewed the distance to the top of the hill with narrowed eyes. "I do not think my ankle is strong enough to go so far."

Eleanor bit back her irritation. "There will be benches on which you can rest."

Reluctantly, Priscilla came along, even took Griff's arm.

He was excessively polite, Eleanor thought. "Would you like to visit the observatory, Lady Priscilla?"

"What is it for?"

"They study the stars."

"No, my ankle is bothering me again. In fact, I think I shall not go any father up the hill."

With great courtesy, Griff offered to escort her back to the boat.

Eleanor could not bear to see her cousin's petulance ruin the afternoon. She stepped close to Priscilla's ear and whispered, "Do not spoil things, my dear. You will disappoint Lord Bromley and Mr. Bates if you make them stop now." Eleanor wanted to give her a sharp pinch but managed to restrain herself.

"I think I can go a bit farther," Priscilla conceded.

Griff took her arm again and led her up the gentle incline, moving more slowly, as though they were all inmates of a hospital for the infirm.

Mr. Bates and Jane walked arm in arm, their happiness evident in every step. Only Priscilla did not notice. Eleanor was relieved their engagement was still a secret, for its announcement would only put her cousin further into her fit of the mopes.

At last, their slow progress reached the top of the hill, and they stood beside the Observatory looking down toward the Thames. The splendor of the panorama before them was truly overwhelming to Eleanor.

Priscilla gave it a glance then sat down on a bench while the rest of them enjoyed the view. Eleanor and Griff exchanged a brief but knowing look.

Jane sounded awestruck. "The Queen's House looks almost exactly like Edenhurst."

"Some say Edenhurst was built first, almost a smaller model of what Jones intended here. Others say Edenhurst came much later, but made use of his experience with the Queen's House and many other buildings."

Eleanor found the vista magnificent. "The positions of the buildings seem carefully arranged to enhance one another!"

Mr. Bates shook his head. "They were done decades apart. Jones started the Queen's House in the early seventeenth century. Wren built the Observatory sixty years later and the Naval Hospital and Chapel even after that. Yet they do all fit together in a most pleasing way."

Eleanor could not take her eyes from the perfection of the view. "From here, the hospital domes frame the view of the river in perfect symmetry with the Queen's House."

Eventually, they started back to the village. When Griff mentioned taking refreshments at an old riverside inn, Priscilla's limp improved markedly. Eleanor and Griff again exchanged a smile, a smile which brought gladness to her heart. She had two problems to solve and then her future looked rosy indeed.

On their second visit to Mrs. Tifton in London, Eleanor and Jane were eager to see Will, their first and favorite student. Mrs. Tifton had arranged a school for him and offered to board him at her house. According to the man who delivered fresh vegetables from the estate to Branden House last week, Will had accompanied him from Hertfordshire that very morning. Now after a few days in town, Eleanor wondered if Will was as enchanted with London as Jane had become.

Will never failed to make them laugh, and today was no exception. At Mrs. Tifton's house, he had constructed a better way to carry the coal upstairs by rigging a pulley to haul a basket from the ground to the first floor. But the children soon turned it into a toy. Disaster struck just before Eleanor and Jane arrived. The children had loaded the cat into the basket, and she jumped out, screeching and hissing, halfway up. Everyone was engaged in a search for the mightily offended feline, but Will paused in his exploration to demonstrate the merit of the arrangement.

At last they settled with Mrs. Tifton in her garden, an oasis of calm amidst beds of daisies. The conversation drifted into a discussion of schools for girls and how they should be taught mathematics and science.

"It is not that I would end the instruction of females in the household arts. Such knowledge is useful to them whether they become mothers or stay unmarried. In fact, I sometimes think we have lost a great deal of knowledge, things that women once knew and no longer do."

Eleanor was intrigued. "What kinds of things to you mean?"

"Sometimes women have a kind of understanding of the world and how people act, well beyond the most scholarly knowledge of the best-educated men. We do not respect the kinds of knowledge women accumulate when they raise their children, sweep the hearth, tend the hens, weed the garden, cook a pot of stew, all at the same time. I believe someday we will respect these many tasks the very humblest women manage."

True, Eleanor thought to herself. *Even a woman like me, with no real purpose to her life, looks for satisfaction and fulfillment.*

"That is an interesting thought," Jane added. "There must be many more accomplishments of traditional women."

"And there are things never discussed in polite society. Foremost among them is the prevention of breeding. There are ways of keeping women from getting with child, ways which allow . . . well, this is an unsuitable subject for young unmarried ladies."

Jane broke into a wide grin. "I will not be unmarried for long. Perhaps this may be knowledge I will need."

Mrs. Tifton hugged her. "Why, Miss Wilson, what happy news. To whom will you be married?"

Jane related all the details, with Eleanor filling in the occasional specific.

Mrs. Tifton asked the question that had been bothering Eleanor. "Miss Milford, what will happen to your school without Miss Wilson?"

Jane answered before Eleanor gave her gloomy assessment. "I have a possible answer for that. When I go home next week, I will talk to Miss Barber. She has often expressed interest in what we do, Eleanor."

To Eleanor this was only a partial solution. "Has Miss Barber any education? She is tied to her mother, is she not?"

"She has education—and wit, too. She was a bright girl, but, beyond attending the academy for two years, she probably knows nothing about the actual classroom experience."

Eleanor gave a shrug. "Neither did I until I had started to teach the children."

Mrs. Tifton assured them she could help. "If Miss Barber is willing, send her to me for a month or two. I will show her what we do here to help teachers. And if she is unable to take over the school, I know of several you might hire."

Eleanor and Jane exclaimed at once.

"What excellent ideas!"

"Oh, thank you. How wonderful!" Wonderful, Eleanor thought to herself, if there was a school at all. The dowager's warning was real. If Priscilla was not betrothed . . . Eleanor dragged her attention back to the conversation.

Jane leaned close to her hostess. "When I move to London, I would hope to spend some time with you myself, Mrs. Tipton."

"You forgot to tell me your husband is a London man."

"My intended also is a teacher, of mapmakers. He is the one with whom we hope Will can study in the future."

"Someday you will have children, is that not so?"

Jane had a dreamy look. "I hope so."

Eleanor admitted a stab of envy. Mrs. Tifton had said her children were a great comfort and reward. No matter how Eleanor loved the children of her school, she could not forever eradicate the appeal of having a few babes of her own.

While Jane and Mrs. Tifton returned to the subject of pregnancy prevention, Eleanor let her mind wander to thoughts of the school. Having a trained teacher would be good for the children. If she should marry, she would no longer live in Branden-under-Wrotham. She would always support her school, but might it be from eighty miles away?

Stop this dreaming, Eleanor! Your first necessity is to ensure the very existence of the school, not spin yourself into your bride clothes!

As they prepared to depart, Mrs. Tifton invited them to a lecture by a leading proponent of educational reform, Mr. MacNeil of Glasgow, a few days hence.

Eleanor agreed. "Jane will have gone home, but I will try to come. I will send word to you if I can attend."

In a flurry of good-byes, they waved to Mrs. Tifton, Will, and her children. To Eleanor, an afternoon dealing with education was a bright beacon in the sea of *ton* events, one almost exactly like another, until the Season ended.

Clarinda, Lady Terrance, sister of Sir Gavin Gawthorpe, stood draped in colorful scarves and many necklaces, her arms adorned with clanking metal bracelets, an unusual sight in a Mayfair drawing room. Griff swallowed his surprise as he waited to greet her, recalling the evening was to include fortune telling by genuine gypsies. Or so they would be called.

When he reached the dimly lit drawing room, he saw several large tents of diaphanous fabric draped from the ceiling. Inside each one, clusters of people stood around fortune tellers seated at little tables. *The measures some people take to attract a crush of visitors to their festivities . . .*

He noticed Eleanor and Priscilla just ahead and caught up with them.

"Ladies, we seem to have arrived at the gypsy camp."

Priscilla squealed in delight. "Is this not too exciting for words? I must know my destiny."

She grabbed his hand and pulled him into one

of the tents where they squeezed into the crowd surrounding a dark haired woman chanting unintelligible words and waving her hands over her glowing crystal ball. Priscilla held tightly to his arm and watched, her eyes large.

"You know this is all nonsense," he murmured in her ear.

"Nonsense?" she whispered back. "These people are mystics. They can foretell the future."

What was the use of going any further, he thought. *Let the girl enjoy the entertainment of the evening.*

Griff looked behind him for Eleanor, but could not find her. Instead, he saw Lord Peters pushing through the crowd to Priscilla.

"Good evening, Lady Priscilla," he said.

"Shhh. I am trying to listen."

Griff and Peters exchanged shrugs. The gypsy woman spoke in a singsong voice. The odor of incense wafted through the tent and made Griff's nose twitch.

Priscilla pressed closer to the table. Sir Gavin, at the front next to the gypsy, pulled her forward.

Griff tried to back away, but those behind him formed a solid wall and he could not move. For the moment, he was stuck listening to this drivel.

Priscilla extended her hand. The woman at the table grabbed it and leaned her face close, as if to study the palm. The gypsy traced shapes on Priscilla's hand, all the while mumbling and making little cries.

The groups around Priscilla pushed forward to hear more, and Griff wondered if the evening's amusements were to include pickpockets. This was a crowd ripe for pilfering.

Again Griff surveyed the faces around him. The

word must have spread quickly that Lady Priscilla was to be the subject of a reading, for he could see most of her admirers nearby.

The gypsy held up her hand for silence. She was obviously skilled at manipulating her audience. "Hear my words, milady. Know what your future is to be. Your palm is rich with hidden meanings." She peered again at Priscilla's hand and pointed to it. "This line speaks of long, long life, and this one of great love."

"Ooooh!" Priscilla glanced around to be sure everyone was listening.

The gypsy kept her head down, probably to keep from laughing, Griff thought.

"You are meant for great achievements, a friendship with royalty, perhaps a marriage of great significance."

Griff almost groaned out loud.

"You will soon make an important decision. I see it coming very soon, within days or weeks."

Or perhaps in a year or two, Griff thought.

The gypsy let go of Priscilla and waved her hands over the crystal ball. "The mystics of the east, the sorcerers of ancient times speak to me." She paused for dramatic effect, casting her eyes upward for a moment, then returning to gaze into the glow of the ball. "I see you will soon find something very valuable."

"What kind of valuable?" Priscilla asked. "Diamonds or money?"

"More precious than gold or jewels. You have had this opportunity before, but passed it by. This time you must recognize it. Take advantage quickly, before your chance is lost forever."

"Oh, what could it be? Love?"

"Perhaps journeys to far-off lands. Perhaps love, milady. There are many men in your aura, but only one who matters."

"Who is he?"

"Ah, the ball grows dim, the spirits depart. I can tell you no more." The woman seemed to go into some sort of trance again, mumbling in some vague syllables.

Griff pretended to laugh, sharing the amusement of the others. But he found the whole performance utterly ridiculous. If he could have gotten away, he would have left the moment it began. As it was, he was now jostled into a group of men, still unable to duck out of the way. They surrounded Priscilla, who had a misty-eyed look, as if she had been truly enchanted.

Sir Gavin took her hand and covered her palm with his. "So much meaning in such a lovely little hand."

Priscilla batted her eyelashes at all of them. "Who is my mystery man? Who is the one that matters?"

"It must be me," Sir Gavin said.

"No, I am the one," someone called.

"Probably Bromley," Lord Peters said.

Griff felt their eyes on him and simply shrugged. Deuce take it, he had to get out of here.

But Priscilla pushed to his side. "Could you be the man, Lord Bromley?"

To Griff's delight, Charlotte Sanderson nearly knocked him off his feet in her rush to reach Priscilla. "Oh, what did she say, dear Priscilla? What did you learn?"

Griff ducked away from the group and did not

stop until he was out of the tented areas and in a second salon, this one far less crowded. *Why was he being so prickly?* This twaddle was exactly what this rout was all about, was it not? The foolishness was what everyone enjoyed. Priscilla was correct, he was a prosy bore.

But it was not the entertainment that bothered him. It was being part of the group bunched around Priscilla. She collected men, then used them as lures to make the others jealous. Of that he'd had quite enough.

He spotted Eleanor on the other side of the room. He lifted two glasses from a tray and approached, presenting her with one of them. "My compliments, Miss Milford."

"Why, how kind of you, Lord Bromley."

They edged away from the others, took positions near a tall portrait of Lady Terrance's father, and pretended to admire the painting.

"Norrie, I have no tolerance for this kind of evening. Your cousin flirts with every man in the room. She does not need me to engender envy in the others. They are competing for her every smile."

"Did you have your future told?"

"Of course I did not! Did you?"

She laughed. "I am about to meet the perfect man."

"How nice for you."

"That fortune teller should have guessed I already know the perfect man."

His fingers itched to touch her, just one little kiss. He wished the room was empty and they were alone so he could take her in his arms. But he stood unmoving. "Quite a coincidence. I happen to know the perfect lady."

She blushed.

"Eleanor, I wonder if you would release me from our plan? I find it impossible to behave as though I were still interested in Priscilla. She has at least seven or eight eager suitors tonight and I . . . I just cannot find the stomach for it anymore."

"Oh, Griff, I watched her silly behavior. I understand how you feel."

"Nor can I hide my feelings when I see you. I think it would be best if I made myself scarce at Branden House for the next few weeks."

"I understand."

"If you need me, Eleanor, you know where I will be—at Bromley House, or perhaps at the club. Bobby needs me, too, for he is in grave danger of falling into a depression now that Jane is gone."

"You are excused, Griff. I will miss seeing you, but it is for the best. For both of us."

He bowed to her. "Make believe I am kissing you, Norrie."

She gazed into his eyes and whispered. "And I am kissing you, too."

Every nerve in his body seemed to sing, as though she was pressed close to him. He could almost feel her moist lips on his, her soft breasts against his chest.

In the midst of the salon, they stood a foot apart, their eyes locked, and pretended to kiss. He had never experienced a more sensual thrill.

Eleven

As she sat in the lecture hall listening to Mr. Mac-Neil, Eleanor's mind kept wandering back to her twin dilemmas. She knew that Griff wanted to make her his wife. She wanted to marry him, of that she had no doubt. But what would happen to Priscilla?

The more difficult predicament was the fate of her school. If she failed to find a match for Priscilla, the dowager wanted to end the school. Now, more than ever, Eleanor felt the need to continue what she and Jane had started. But how?

Jane's letter told of her successful recruitment of Miss Barber to teach at their school. The lady was delighted, Jane wrote, to have an undertaking besides the care of her invalid mother. Miss Barber had already found a village woman to tend her mother every morning.

The dowager's cooperation would be essential for continuation. And that meant . . .

Eleanor tried to concentrate on the speaker's words. Mr. MacNeil advocated expert teachers trained in techniques of which she had never heard. Jane, she mused, had a natural talent for reaching children. She herself had some ability, though from whence it came, Eleanor had no idea. Whether Miss Barber had a similar aptitude was a good question.

She glanced around the room. The rows of chairs were full of respectably dressed people, not one of whom she knew. But as the applause died away at the end of Mr. MacNeil's talk, many came up to Mrs. Tifton to exchange pleasantries.

Leaving the hall, Eleanor's head spun from all the introductions she experienced. She probably would not remember a single one if she met any of them again. She wished Mrs. Tifton a pleasant farewell at the corner, where her carriage awaited.

When she walked into Branden House, all Eleanor wanted was a soothing rest before preparing for the evening's dinner and ball at Lady Smallwood's. Lady Smallwood had a daughter whose envy of Priscilla was well known. Eleanor would have to keep a close eye on her cousin to prevent any missteps the Smallwoods might use to trigger gossip.

Plus, Eleanor wanted very much to sit down and think about all the things she had learned at the lecture. Even though she had often been thinking of her personal concerns, she wanted to reflect on Mr. Mac-Neil's ideas about training teachers.

But when she entered her room, Priscilla's maid waited, wringing her hands and looking near tears.

"What can I do for you, Mary?"

"I was puttin' out Lady Priscilla's gown, 'n I seen she had moved some of 'em. So I looked through 'er wardrobe. Oh, Miss Eleanor, some of 'er things are gone, and all 'er jewelry too. Unless I don't know where t' look. Or I am losin' my mind?"

By the time the maid had blurted out the words, Eleanor had forgotten the lecture, forgotten the quiet time she craved. Her heart pounded, and she rushed to Priscilla's room to see the maid's evidence.

"I hope you are right and she has moved her things, but I doubt it. Let me take a quick look, and then we will see what we can find."

Only a glance was necessary to see that Priscilla's best gowns were missing. "When did you last see her?"

"Not since early morning. What 're we to do?"

"Have you spoken to the duchess?"

"Not yet. I 'magine she's restin.'"

"Have you asked anyone else?"

"No, ma'am. I jes' discovered it a while ago."

"And you are certain no one else has missed her?"

"Not as I know."

"Thank you, Mary. Please stay here in Lady Priscilla's bedchamber. Ah, count up all her stockings and gloves. Make an inventory so we can tell what is missing." Keeping her busy and away from the other servants seemed wise.

"Yes, ma'am."

"Say nothing to a soul. Lady Priscilla will be back shortly, and we do not want to disturb anyone, especially the duchess." Eleanor wished she felt the confidence she tried to show Mary.

"Yes, ma'am."

The last thing they needed was some hysterical servant or the duchess howling for a city-wide search.

Eleanor returned to her bedchamber and stared out the window. Obviously Priscilla was gone, but where? If, God forbid, she was eloping, she could have had hours on the road already.

Eleanor needed to send for Griff, much as she hated to interfere in his self-imposed exile from Priscilla's company. He would know what to do. He would know how to deal with the elopement or the

abduction or whatever it turned out to be. And she
had no time to lose.

She dashed to the library and wrote a brief note,
then summoned a footman. "Run to Bromley House
as fast as your feet will carry you. If Lord Bromley is
not there, try White's."

The footman bowed, tucked the note in his waistcoat, and strode off toward the rear entrance.

Eleanor sank into a chair and put her face in her
hands. Why had she not seen this coming? She had
no idea what Priscilla was thinking these days. No,
Eleanor had been so selfishly concerned with her own
renewed love for Griff she had forgotten about most
of her duties as a chaperon. After all, she was not just
to find a match but also to tend to Priscilla's behavior.
A good chaperon would have kept herself informed
of which men her charge favored, made certain all
of them were aware of her standards of behavior.

She stood and began to pace from one end of the
long empty drawing room to the other. The once
proper Miss Milford had allowed herself to slack off,
to betray herself and Priscilla. She deserved every
scrap of disgrace attached to this calamity. She could
almost hear the duke, then her grandmother.

Which meant her school was finished, if Grandmother had her way. "Oh, poor Miss Barber . . ."

Back and forth she paced. Her thoughts flitted in a
dozen directions. The ormolu clock chimed the hour.
What time had she sent the footman? Had it been a
quarter hour ago or more? How much longer would
it take for Griff get here? But what if he was not home
or at his club? He might be anywhere.

She never should have gone to that meeting. She
should have been more cautious. It was all her fault.

Why had she not suspected Priscilla would take an opportunity to escape? But with whom? Eleanor should have known, should have paid more attention to the girl. For all of several months now, the Prima had hidden her headstrong nature under a façade of cooperation and sweetness. Make that sham cooperation and false sweetness.

She reached the end of the room and turned back for at least the twentieth time, telling herself she was a fool, a gull too easily taken in. What if Priscilla were on her way to Gretna Green?

To Eleanor, it seemed as though several hours passed before Griff hurried in, his face showing his concern. "Your note said an urgent matter. How can I help?"

Eleanor tried to remain calm, remain logical, but she was near tears and feeling miserable by the time she finished the story of Priscilla's disappearance.

Griff narrowed his eyes and stroked his chin, walked over to the window and stared out on the square, saying nothing. His face was impassive, his expression unreadable.

What could he be thinking? Eleanor wanted to shake him. Hurry, she wanted to shout. *Do not stand looking out the window. Do something!* But she remained quiet, letting him think.

When he finally cleared his throat as if to speak, she was nearly mad with worry.

"I suspect she is not on the way to Gretna Green. I could be mistaken, of course, but I suspect we will find her at Blythe's house not two streets away."

"You think Lord Blythe abducted her? But she packed her gowns and jewelry as if she was running away."

"He probably lied to her. He is not to be trusted. I

should have told all of you long before this. If I have
correctly identified the circumstance, I blame myself."

"But why would he not immediately flee to Scotland with her?"

"It is known in the clubs that the duke, your uncle,
has not settled a specific amount on Lady Priscilla as
dowry. All assume he will choose an amount only
when the betrothal is contracted. If Blythe married
her without Lawrence's approval, the dowry might be
nothing. But if he ruins her, or threatens to do so, he
might be able to negotiate a large cash settlement,
which he badly needs."

"But what can we do?"

"I shall go immediately to his house and demand
her release."

"Do you think he will just give her up without a fuss?"

"I do not know."

"I must come with you. If she is frightened, she may
need me. I have been thinking for the last half hour
of all the things I should have recognized. Her behavior has been very bad in several recent events. I
should have been more aware and alert."

"Do not be silly. You cannot blame yourself. You are
blameless. She is a young woman quite aware of her
powers."

"But—"

"We are wasting time. We must go quickly to Blythe's
residence."

Griff's carriage waited outside Branden House. As
they drove the short distance to Blythe's, Eleanor
tried to tell Griff the layout of the house as she knew
it from a dinner party she had attended there weeks

ago. "I never believed I would go there on a mission to rescue anyone. I just recall the library is to the right and the drawing room up one flight."

When a perfectly correct butler answered the door, Griff shoved his way inside. Eleanor hurried after him.

The butler sputtered at both of them. "His lordship is not at home." He put out an arm to restrain Griff.

Eleanor gave a loud moan and launched herself at the butler, forcing him to catch her. Griff lunged up the stairs two at a time and shouted for Blythe.

Eleanor whimpered and lolled back in the butler's arms. "I need tea. Or a brandy." She moaned again until she saw indecision on the man's face. She heard Griff pounding on a distant door. The butler led her to a chair and headed for the service door.

As soon as he was gone, Eleanor ran up the staircase two flights to the bedrooms. Panting and breathless, she tried the doors of several rooms opening off the main corridor. Her heart raced as fast as her breathing. When she found a locked door, she called out. "Priscilla, are you in there?"

"Eleanor. Thank God you have come! He made me his prisoner in here."

Eleanor took a deep breath and steadied herself against the doorjamb. "Let me see if I can find a key."

Eleanor looked under the edge of the rug, then on the hall table. The key sat beside a dusty clock. She grabbed it, jammed it into the lock, and turned it quickly.

When the door swung open, Eleanor was prepared to take a frightened Priscilla in her arms and wipe away her sorry tears. She was not prepared to find a woman as angry as a drenched cat and pouring out an angry tirade against Blythe.

"The scurrilous knave tricked me! I cannot believe I was such a gudgeon. I had faith in his story. But as soon as we came here, the wretch changed everything."

"Priscilla, are you all right?"

"Oh, I would not let the muckworm touch me. I told him I would scratch his eyes out."

"So you are unhurt?"

"Why did I believe him, Eleanor? The dastard promised me a trip to Paris and then he said he would have to have my marriage settlement first."

"Where are your things, your jewelry?"

"I do not know about the baggage, but I have the jewelry in my reticule. It is very heavy and I hit him with it. He will never have a penny from us, and not a single piece to pawn, either."

Eleanor hugged Priscilla. "You may have made a dreadful mistake, Priscilla, but you have handled yourself in an exemplary fashion in the face of that error."

"How did you find me? Blythe said no one would ever know where I was. Or that you would send a dozen riders to Scotland."

"Lord Bromley suspected Blythe was not all he should be, where honor and respect are concerned."

"Lord Bromley? Oh, Eleanor, I know he is a man of honor. Where is he?"

"Downstairs. Facing Blythe, I assume, from the voices I heard when I came up here."

Priscilla smoothed back her hair. "I hope they are not fighting. Or that one of them has a pistol."

Quietly they stole down the stairs and headed for the sound of the angry voices.

Griff's voice was steely with determination. "You are finished, Blythe. Done with England."

Priscilla did not hesitate to burst into the room. "You lying blackguard!"

Griff caught her arm before she reached Blythe. "Wait, Priscilla. He will not try to hurt you anymore."

"No, but I intend to hurt him. My father will have the callous brute horsewhipped. Or worse."

Blythe's face showed his scorn. "Tell that silly chit to pipe down."

Priscilla set her arms akimbo. "No one speaks to me like that, you scoundrel."

"If you had just an ounce of understanding, we could have had a perfectly agreeable arrangement, my pet. But you—"

"When you said marriage and Gretna Green in the same breath, you toadeater, what was I to think? Then there was no carriage waiting to dash to the border. Nothing you promised happened!"

Griff intervened. "That is quite enough from both of you. Priscilla, I am sending you and Eleanor home in my carriage."

"Take her," Blythe said. "I am well rid of the chit."

Griff ignored him. "Then I will have my driver come back and take Blythe and me on a little jaunt to Dover, where I will see him on a packet to France, from which he will return at the risk of being made a laughing-stock and losing any shred of reputation he ever had." Griff stared him in the eye. "The Peninsula incident, for example, could interest a number of people."

Eleanor was about to endorse the plan when Priscilla suddenly cried out.

"Oh, what about Charlotte?"

"Charlotte?" they asked in chorus.

"Charlotte is supposed to tell everyone tonight at the Smallwood's ball. Oh, Lord, I am ruined!"

Eleanor felt her stomach heave.

Blythe burst into laughter.

Griff was not amused. "Stow it."

Blythe turned his laugh into a sort of throat-clearing cough.

Her fists clenched, Priscilla looked ready to commit murder if she could find a weapon.

Griff looked at Eleanor. "Is there anything we can do?"

She shrugged. "Let me think a moment."

"Don't leave me alone with that hellcat," Blythe said.

Griff chuckled. "Perhaps that is a better solution. Or you two could go to the ball and prove Miss Sanderson's story wrong."

Eleanor nodded. "That is almost right. I say we all go to the ball together."

Priscilla's face was livid. "What are you talking about? Everyone will think I have married Blythe."

"Not for long. And especially not if you enter on Lord Bromley's arm. And I am escorted by . . ." Eleanor took a deep breath. "Lord Blythe."

Griff agreed. "Precisely, Miss Milford."

"But I do not want to be within ten yards of that blackguard," Priscilla said.

Eleanor wished she could shake the girl. "Then think of a better way to prevent a scandal."

"All agreed, Priscilla and Norrie?" Griff asked. "You have no vote, Blythe."

Slowly, Priscilla nodded. "I agree."

Griff rubbed his hands together. "This caper, then, is not over yet. We will all put on our best evening dress and go to Lady Smallwood's ball. Together. Call your man, Blythe. I will accompany you to make sure you do not try to crawl out of the window. When you are dressed for the ball, we will take the ladies to Branden House and then go to my rooms. Don't think you can get away, either. You don't want the *ton* to know this story any more than Priscilla does."

An hour later, Eleanor scuttled her repugnance and took Lord Blythe's arm as they stood in the foyer of the Smallwood residence. Eleanor held her head high and pasted a smile on her face as they preceded Priscilla and Griff into the ballroom. Eleanor tried to ignore the many heads that swiveled their way as their names were announced.

Blythe was grinning like a cat approaching a nest of helpless baby sparrows.

Eleanor had never felt more conspicuous, but she forced herself to nod and smile at acquaintances. All the time her hand, even within her glove, burned from the distasteful contact with Blythe's forearm.

Blythe looked down at her and smiled. "You amaze me, Miss Milford."

She kept her voice soft, for his ear only. "No, Blythe, you are the amazing one. To have imagined you could bend Priscilla to your wishes. How little insight you gained, even after spending so many hours in her company." Eleanor broke off and smiled to Mrs. Shepperly, whose face held a look of total bewilderment.

Eleanor hated every moment of the charade. But she had to do it. She had to make people believe she was interested in Lord Blythe. Why could she not call up a blush, bring her cheeks to pink when she wanted to? Those occasions when she wanted to be cool and distant, then felt her face reddening, were so embarrassing. Now when she needed one of those silly flushes, it was not to be.

Eleanor dipped her chin and gazed up at Blythe,

forcing her lips to curve into a smile. He grinned back as though he truly had designs upon her. She had to clamp her teeth together to keep from sputtering aloud. What, indeed, did he have in mind?

She took a deep breath as she swept her gaze downward and to the side in what she hoped was a flirtatious and encouragingly coy move. At the very edge of her peripheral vision, she could see Mrs. Bentley-Morgan's forehead crinkle into a little frown.

Blythe cupped his hand around her elbow and steered her toward the balcony, but she swerved a little to the right, stopped near Lady Belfour, and gave a little curtsy. "Good evening, Lady Belfour. I believe you are acquainted with Lord Blythe?"

Lady Belfour smiled but her eyes remained as cold and hard as solid ice. "Good evening, Eleanor, Lord Blythe."

He bowed and gave his widest grin, all that was proper on the surface. Eleanor felt her cheek muscles ache with the tension of maintaining her smile.

When they went into the supper room, Eleanor could at last move a few feet away from Blythe, who nevertheless insisted upon arranging a plate for her, with the most spurious solicitude she could imagine.

They avoided most of the crowd and sat alone in a corner, out of the hearing of the others. He actually seemed to be enjoying the evening's charade.

"My dear Eleanor, your cousin is a young lady of rare temper."

"I am glad to hear it." She gave him a sweet smile, the first sincere one of the night. "Priscilla is a young lady who knows what she wants, and, Lord Blythe"—she broadened her smile—"I do not believe that what she wants is you, however you have tried to mislead her."

Blythe snorted in disdain. "She is not without her refined qualities, however. You may be interested to know that when I offered her a lovely necklace of diamonds and sapphires, she immediately held it up to the light, examined it closely, and declared the jewels were simply glass."

Eleanor did not suppress her chuckle. "Priscilla is well educated about the value of gemstones. Of that you may be certain."

"As a matter of fact, I consider myself quite fortunate to be rescued by you and Lord Bromley. You had no idea who actually needed rescuing in the situation."

Eleanor's laughter was genuine. "Priscilla will make the right gentleman an excellent wife. Her fashion sense is unerring; she understands the importance of appearance in Society. She will be a fine hostess for her husband, and I doubt she will meddle in political matters, except to charm every member of the government whose favor her husband is seeking."

In fact, Eleanor thought, she would be a perfect wife for a man of property. She was capable of the greatest charm to the tenants at her father's estate and she knew precisely how to deal with large numbers of servants. Indeed, she might be an ideal wife, assuming they were successful in diverting the scandal tonight. And found the right husband for her.

She looked over at Priscilla, who looked entirely comfortable, smiling to everyone, just as though she had no idea that a plethora of conflicting stories were passing from person to person through the assembly. Too bad, Eleanor thought, that a career on the stage was impossible for a respectable young lady, for Priscilla certainly had a great deal of acting talent. She smiled at Griff, as though she were completely in love.

After they ate, Lord Blythe bowed to Priscilla and led her onto the floor for a set of country dances.

Eleanor did not take her eyes off them. They looked quite normal. Surprisingly so. Amazingly so. Could Blythe still be thinking of grabbing her from beneath their eyes?

Griff joined her on the sidelines. "I believe we have passed the most difficult tests."

"Thank heavens. Though from the look on his face, he might try to spirit her away again right before our eyes. Could that be possible?"

"I would be surprised if he attempted anything. He has no resources. His household has probably been without wages for a long time, and I assume he owes his bookmaker, tailor, and many, many others."

Eleanor glanced quickly at Griff. "Why does he not pay? I thought he had a handsome fortune."

"So he would have Society believe, but I have looked into his affairs. He is a complete fake, other than holding a minor title without real property. He may have better luck with his pretenses abroad. By the way, Norrie, your aptitude for the strategic swoon was extremely well done this afternoon."

She felt the blush she had sought an hour ago. "Thank you, my lord. It was all I could do in the circumstances."

"I admire your quick thinking."

Eleanor watched with relief as Priscilla was sought out by other gentleman to go to the dance floor. Eleanor danced as well, not only with Blythe, and by the wee hours, her feet ached. She kept a smile on her face and found chatter to share with every partner, though she yearned for the moment she too could escape the ballroom.

At last, Griff called for his carriage and escorted Eleanor and Priscilla down the stairway to pick up their wraps, then into the carriage. Two of the Bromley footmen, burly fellows, stood by. Blythe waited without offering his farewells, now a virtual prisoner of Lord Bromley.

Griff leaned into the carriage. "I will see you the day after tomorrow when I have returned from Dover. Blythe knows he is getting off easy, so I anticipate no further trouble. Good night."

Both Eleanor and Priscilla gave their thanks and, as the horses pulled away from the Smallwoods' house, they sighed together.

Priscilla put her concerns into questions. "Did we do it? Were people convinced? Did we manage to escape a scandal?"

Eleanor sighed. "I believe so, but we will know more after tomorrow's round of visitors. We will have a houseful of curious callers."

"I do not know if I can bear it."

"We shall have to prepare Violet."

"Oh, no! Eleanor, if we tell her, she will tell Father, and I will be in the soup for certain."

"We need only say that a host of rumors were circulating. I hope you spoke to Charlotte tonight and told her it was all a silly hum."

"That is precisely what I did. I said I was only teasing, but I do not know if she believed me."

"As long as she never knows the truth."

"How will I be able to talk to everyone tomorrow?"

"You must," Eleanor said. "You did very well tonight, and you will manage tomorrow's callers with the same charm and grace."

Priscilla's eyes glittered in the light from the lamp

inside the carriage. "I will do my best. Now, Eleanor, give me your honest opinion. Do you think I still might be able to snare Lord Bromley? I admire him more than I can say."

Eleanor feared she might succumb to the emotions of the trying day and burst into tears. But she managed to keep her composure. "I thought you had definitely decided that Lord Bromley was too old and too boring for you."

"But he is strong and brave, and I think I am in love with him now. Perhaps it took a crisis to see the truth. Is that not what the poets say?"

"No line carrying that thought occurs to me at the moment, Priscilla."

"Remember what the fortune teller said? I had missed one good opportunity, but I would have another chance. I think the gypsy meant my romance with Lord Bromley."

"I am sure we are both too tired to think straight. Are you not eager for rest?"

"I am only eager for tomorrow to pass and the next day to arrive when I will see Bromley again. I am sure I can win his regard. I will have Violet send for him. That is, if I survive the harpies and their nosy questions. I must do it, for him. For Bromley, my darling."

Eleanor closed her eyes and said no more.

Twelve

"My lord."

Griff knew it was the third repetition by Bellows, but he could not seem to struggle out of a state of sleep.

He opened one eye. "Yes?"

"My lord, Miss Milford has come to call.

"What's the time?"

"It lacks a few moments of eight in the morning."

Griff groaned. He had not returned from Dover until almost seven. But Norrie was below, and she would not have come unless it was urgent.

"Tell her I will join her in a quarter hour."

Eleanor had received the news from Bellows with disappointment. She hoped to intercept Griff before he slept, but clearly she had been too late. His most efficient butler had awakened him, and now that his slumber was interrupted, she had no choice but to wait for him to come down.

She sipped the coffee Bellows served her in the quiet drawing room and thought about her choice for Priscilla.

Yesterday's callers had filled Branden House. Despite their fears, Eleanor and Priscilla countered every stray rumor about Lord Blythe, about Priscilla, about Charlotte. If the visitors were not fully convinced, at least they had presented a unified position.

Except for the part about Griff. To Eleanor's chagrin, Priscilla had dropped a host of broad hints of her adoration for Lord Bromley and her hopes for a forthcoming offer of marriage.

Now, telling Griff before he encountered any of the gossip was essential. And she needed him to help carry out her plan.

When Griff arrived, he wore a dressing gown and his chin showed a faint shadow of beard. "Forgive my lack of proper attire, Norrie. But I assume your mission is urgent."

Eleanor stood awkwardly and tried to smile, but her attempt felt like a grimace. "I had hoped to catch you upon your return before you slept. I apologize for coming here and upsetting the household. I need to speak to you in private, and . . . this is very complicated."

"Please sit, Norrie. I am pleased to see you any time, my dear."

She sat on the settee and he took a chair across from her.

"I am at your service."

"Again. I am sorry to be such a nuisance, Griff, but . . ." She let her voice trail off.

He reached over and took her hand. "You will never be a nuisance to me."

"Thank you again for your kindness to Priscilla and to me."

"It is not necessary to thank me. Getting that slimy Blythe out of the country is more than enough recompense for my meager activities."

"So he is gone for good?"

"I listed the things I would do to him if I ever heard he returned to England. He knows a smattering of the Portuguese tongue, so I expect he will head for Brazil."

Eleanor took a deep breath. "Griff, your heroism has impressed Priscilla. She is now quite convinced that you are the perfect gentleman for her. You will receive a summons from the duchess, today I believe, and she will offer you Priscilla's hand in marriage."

With some satisfaction and relief, she watched the frown mount his forehead. "What?"

"Priscilla hatched this plan yesterday before the callers arrived. When they came, she hinted to everyone that she is in love and has settled on you. She will do anything to guarantee your immediate offer."

Griff shook his head as if not comprehending her words. For long moments he said nothing, simply stared at the floor. "Can we change her mind?"

"That is the question. For the moment, you are the man of her heart."

"Is there some new fellow to dangle before her, someone who has not been around for the Season?"

"Perhaps, but I do not want to take any chances, Griff. If my idea is successful, she will be betrothed right away. That is, unless you want to marry her after all."

Griff stared at her for a moment before breaking into a grin and speaking in a teasing tone. "I have expectations of marrying into the Duke of Branden's family, but my choice is not Priscilla."

"Oh, Griff, I hoped . . ." She began, then hesitated and flinched at her own cowardice. "I have something very important to tell you." The words were almost blurted out, without grace or even a hint of a smile.

She stopped and breathed deeply, looking at him to see only a puzzled glint in his eyes. "Oh, this is very difficult."

"Yes, Norrie, what is it?"

"Back in the maze, I thought we needed to wait, wait until Priscilla was betrothed. Now I think that was a mistake." Her voice had grown hollow to her own ears. She stopped and stared at the floor, afraid to look at him. "I seem to make too many mistakes where you are concerned, Griff. I was wrong to delay." She stood and faced him. "Oh, I love you, Griff."

At once he was beside her, turning her shoulders and taking her into his arms. "My darling, Norrie, you know I could never marry Priscilla. I want to marry you."

Eleanor leaned against his chest and listened to the thump of his heartbeat. Her own was racing like the wind.

They stood locked together for a moment. Then he pulled back and led her to the settee. "Tell me the rest of it, Norrie. What you think we should do, I mean."

"We must find a way to divert Priscilla's attention and find her another gentleman to occupy her thoughts and her fancies."

"Anyone but me. She has rooms full of attentive men following her every move. Does she seem to favor the older fellows or the callow youths?"

"She has wanted simply to collect as many ad-mirers as possible, but I feel her ideas have changed. She has told me from the start that she wished to be betrothed at the end of the Season, just as our grandmother wishes. Priscilla would rather not return to Branden, at least not for long."

"How does the duchess feel about that?"

"Nothing would please Violet more than to have Priscilla out from under her feet."

"So tell me, Norrie, if you and I were to announce our betrothal, would not the responsibility of finding a match for Priscilla fall on Violet's shoulders? If she wants her stepdaughter away from her house, she would have to put herself to work on the problem."

"That is hopeless! And if I intend to have the school, we have to find the match, not leave it to Violet. Let me tell you about my plan."

Griff and Lord Arlford sat in a quiet corner of the coffee room, where the waiter filled their glasses with claret and left the bottle beside them.

"From the evidence of last evening, I deduce I am to wish you happy, Bromley."

"The situation is not quite what it seems." Griff gave a little laugh. "In fact you can wish me happy, but not with the lady you suppose I favor."

"Is that so?"

"Yes, though for the moment, I ask you not to mention this to anyone. Miss Milford is the lady who has consented to be my wife."

Arlford straightened up like a jack-in-the-box. "Eleanor Milford?"

"Indeed. And I am the most fortunate of all men to have won her affection."

"Damn if it did not appear otherwise! What was Blythe in all of that? At Smallwood's, it looked like he might be altar bound with Miss Milford, with you close on his heels with Lady Priscilla. Came perilously close to breaking my son's heart."

"Which is precisely what I want to discuss with you."

Arlford took several swallows of his wine. "All Season Charles has been hankering after Lady Priscilla, though he claimed he was interested only in leaving the country. Why, I cannot fathom. No sense at all in fiddling with foreigners. Has all he needs right here."

"I think I have a measure of understanding of Lord Peters's wanderlust. I base this on our conversations in the last few months, though I expect my impressions are also affected by what I have heard from other young men."

"I should like to hear your views, Bromley."

"My brother was much the same. As the heir to a title, just like your son, he was unable to go off and do what so many of his friends and schoolmates did, that is, fight with Wellington, or somehow do his part. I was luckier for a good many years. I went to Portugal. Though any man who has experienced war can tell you it is filthy, tragic, and brings out the worst in men, there is also a measure of comradeship and accomplishment that can satisfy the drive of a young man."

"I have heard others voice similar opinions, though I cannot comprehend wanting to kill."

"Oh, I could not agree more. But there are many aspects to war besides killing. And many who find those parts of service rewarding."

"Go on." Arlford rubbed his chin.

"When you were a lad, some of those desires for adventure of young men were met by the Grand Tour, traveling across the Alps and into new circumstances. This, I believe is what Lord Peters craves."

Arlford sat in silence for a few moments. "That is all well and good. But I am not a healthy man. Charles is my only son, and I wish to see him married and a father before I turn up my toes. I fear there is not time for him to lollygag around Germany or prance around Rome. But the boy has no interest in my opinion. Instead of looking for a biddable miss, he has trailed after the Season's belle, Lady Priscilla. Took his place with the bunch of you sniffing around her and now he is as damned foolish as those crazy poets that extol a broken heart. By God, it makes me want to take the switch to him like his tutor did a dozen or more years ago."

Griff wondered if the older man was listening. His eyes had a faraway look that seemed to indicate he was unreachable.

The silence lengthened until Lord Arlford picked up his glass and drained it, smacking it down on the table and filling it again. "By God, I do not understand it."

"Sir, Miss Milford and I had an idea we wanted to suggest to you."

"Yes?"

"If Lady Priscilla were to consent to wed your son, what would you think of sending the pair of them off to Italy? A kind of extended wedding trip . . ."

Lord Arlford shook his head in despair.

"Are you trying to rattle me with over the moon

plans like that? Would Lady Priscilla give Charles a second glance?"

"I have reason to believe she would, though I am not certain where her heart is. I know I did not engage her affections. She is much like Charles in many ways, young and fresh, but also looking for independence, for a life of her own, for experience and even adventure. A dreamer. It seems to me that sharing such a trip would bring them close together. They might not be in love at this precise moment, but after a few months under the sunshine and moonbeams of Italy, how could they be otherwise?"

Lord Arlford looked thoughtful. "My man of business has just announced his wedding plans. If I sent him and his bride along to guide Charles and Priscilla . . ."

"Just caution them not to spend too much time looking at architecture."

Priscilla moped in her bedroom until early afternoon, when Eleanor decided that she had waited long enough to have her most important talk with her cousin.

"Come," Priscilla answered to her tapping on the door.

"How do you feel today?" Eleanor asked.

"I would feel fine if I was not so mad. Why did Blythe promise . . . oh, he is an awful man."

"I entirely agree. You had a narrow escape and you are very lucky indeed."

"But in just a few weeks I will go home again with Violet. I can hardly imagine a worse fate. I may have been declared a Toast by some people, but I have not found a single gentleman I want to marry."

"I know what I would do if I were you."

"Tell me."

Eleanor leaned close. "I would think about the gypsy's words."

"That I would have another opportunity?"

"No. I mean the part about traveling to exotic lands. You know that very nice young man Lord Peters will be a marquess someday."

"He goes on and on about Italy . . ."

"And would you not like to visit there?"

"Of course I would. The carnival in Venice sounds more exciting than a Shakespeare ball, that is certain. And even though we were supposed to hate Napoleon, I have always wanted to go to Paris."

"If you were to marry Lord Peters, I wonder if you could have a wedding trip to Paris."

Priscilla sat up straighter and looked thoughtful. "For Paris I might marry a coachman."

Eleanor giggled. "More likely if you married a coachman, you would see nothing more than the Great North Road, up which your father would send you to stay forever."

Priscilla joined in the laughter. "To see his face and Grandmother's! It might be worth the risk."

"So that is the real reason you tried to run off with Blythe!"

Priscilla's face fell. "I may not be clever, or smart like you or Jane Wilson. But I did not believe I was stupid or a fool. Yes, he treated me like I was a witless chit without a grain of sense. How could I have believed what he said? I was a mindless henwit!"

Eleanor patted her cousin's hand. "Do not berate

yourself, Priscilla. You did not allow him to have his way with you. You showed ingenuity and gumption. And I am proud of you. I will never tell your story to her, but your grandmother would be proud of you, too."

"Grandmother?"

"She admires a woman with backbone, you know."

"Oh, Eleanor, please do not tell her. I still feel such a fool."

Eleanor wanted to bring the topic back to Lord Peters. "Lord Peters is a charming young man. It is sad that he lost his mother so many years ago."

"I like his father. He is a courteous man."

"They say that most young men as they grow older turn out to be very much like their fathers."

"Do you really think I should marry Charles? He is a nice fellow, but I never thought he really was interested in me. He seemed like he was only crazy about Italy and France."

"I have it on good authority that he has been captivated by you from the very first. And now I suggest you get yourself ready for another afternoon of callers. Perhaps Lord Peters will come, and you want to look your very best."

After leaving Priscilla, hoping she had planted the right ideas and that Griff had been even more effective with Lord Arlford, Eleanor visited Violet.

"How are you feeling today? You must have had a bad night."

"I never have a good night anymore."

"I hope you are not feverish, for your cheeks look a bit redder than usual."

"Oh, bring me a mirror, please, Eleanor. Let me look."

Eleanor walked to the dressing table and picked up a hand mirror. "Oh, I am sure it is nothing, my dear. Just my imagination, I am certain."

"No, no! You are correct. I am flushed indeed. Please call for my maid. And perhaps you should send for Mr. Weems."

"Why not try a sleeping draught? You will feel better after a good rest."

"I am certain you are correct. You are so thoughtful, Eleanor."

"If when you awake, if you still want Mr. Weems, I will send for him immediately."

She tiptoed away as Violet closed her eyes and fanned her cheeks.

Two hours later, the Marquess of Arlford and his son arrived at Branden House. Only two ladies, both friends of the dowager, had come to call. Both of them were considerably interested in seeing the two gentlemen come into the drawing room.

Eleanor felt a bit pushy as she stood and waved her hand toward the door, saying, "How very nice of you to call, Lady Simtsen and Mrs. Rutledge. I hope we shall see you soon over the card table."

Both ladies rose, perhaps reluctantly, and moved toward the door, looking over their shoulders, obviously wishing they could stay.

When she came back into the drawing room, Lord Arlford beckoned her to his side as he stood at the window, well away from the other two occupants of the room. "I wish we might leave the room in a moment or two, Miss Milford."

She stole a glance at the sofa, where Priscilla was leaning toward Lord Peters and hanging on his every word. It looked very promising.

"Lord Arlford, I recently found an atlas in the library that is almost two hundred years old."

"I should like to see it."

"Then, come along. We can look at it now. Please excuse us, Priscilla, Lord Peters. If you need us, we will be in the duke's library."

"Nicely done, Miss Milford." Lord Arlford chuckled as they crossed the corridor.

The Dowager Duchess of Branden sat between Lord Arlford and Lady Edenhurst. The ballroom was elegantly festooned in billows of white silk, more extravagant by far than that used by Eleanor for Priscilla's ball.

The dowager's sons, the duke and his brother Lord Harley, were prepared to celebrate the betrothals of their daughters, Lady Priscilla and Miss Milford. Violet, who had made the ultimate effort to hold up the family's honor, as she told them over and over again, was delighted to take all the credit for arranging the successful conclusion of the Season with the victorious celebratory results. "My health may suffer for months, but I am so gratified I could assist the young ladies to conclude their matches. It was my pleasure and my privilege, of course, no matter the cost to my delicate nerves and my continual megrims."

Eleanor stood on the sidelines, wishing the announcements and toasts were over and done with. Griff was busy keeping Lord Peters from succumbing to a case of nerves, while Jane sat next to Mr. Bates and gazed into his eyes. Theirs was the third betrothal of the Season for Branden House, and the announcement had already been posted and the banns read. Jane would be the first bride of the trio. Priscilla would be next, at St. George's, Hanover Square, followed by a magnificent breakfast right here at Branden House.

Griff and Eleanor would celebrate their nuptials at the tiny church in Bromley a few days later, a modest ceremony followed by a festive dinner for all the Edenhurst tenants.

Eleanor looked at the priceless rope of pearls, the choice of a bridal gift she had made from the dowager's collection. Priscilla chose a sapphire tiara, which sparkled all the way across the room. Eleanor looped the pearls over her fingers.

"Stop that!" The dowager appeared at her side. "Twisting pearls will cause them to break."

"Yes, grandmother. I promise to leave them alone, for they are truly beautiful and I love them."

"Of course they are beautiful. I chose them sixty years ago because they were so lovely. Take care of them."

"I shall."

"If you go off to live in Sussex, Eleanor, what will become of your school? That Wilson girl is not going to be around either, I hear."

"I have made arrangements for a teacher to come from Mrs. Tifton's training program in London. He will be assisted by Miss Barber from Branden-under-Wrotham."

"And how will he be paid?"

"From my mother's legacy. I consider your endowment of the building and its care to be complete fulfillment of our bargain, Grandmother. I would not expect you to pay the teacher too."

"Tell me, Eleanor, does that Bromley fellow know what a needlewit he is going to marry? Some men don't appreciate a woman with brains, you know."

"Oh, Grandmother, when it comes to my feelings for Lord Bromley, if you knew how many mistakes I have made, you would say I was the flightiest shatterbrain in the realm!"

AUTHOR'S NOTE

My great-great-great-grandfather Edward Barnard Metcalf was baptized in St. Andrew Undershaft, London, in 1783. He married Maria Sully in Hackney Parish in 1810. Their first child, Ann Isabel Reynolds Metcalf, was born in Portugal, where Edward served as a royal engineer. My great-great-grandfather, Arthur Edward Metcalf, was born in 1822, the second son. Arthur came to Albion, Illinois, in 1839 to farm his father's land near the Wabash River at the edge of the great prairie.

In 2001, cousin Shera Biggers Thompson and I found a dozen of Edward Barnard Metcalf's exquisitely drawn signed maps at the Public Records Office, Kew. Several dated from his service in the Peninsula, others from Belgium, and the remainder from his surveys of English counties.

More Regency Romance From Zebra